PUFFIN BOOKS

ALLY, ALLY, AS̶

Richard Pledge did not w̶̶̶
door. It was bad enough t̶̶̶ ̶ ̶ ̶̶
new neighbours on lovely, ̶ ̶ ̶ House
Moor, without having to tak̶ ̶ ̶ ̶ ̶is wing the
wispy, pale, pathetic little Ally. Mum said she had
a sad history, and should be befriended. Richard
resisted – somehow he knew it would be better to
leave well alone. That autumn Richard tried hard
to stay out of trouble. He ignored the strange
hints about Ally from his friend Dr Radleigh, he
restrained his sister's fantasies about kidnapped
heiresses and wicked guardians. But Laura's fantasies got wilder, and more sinister . . . Shadows
of witchcraft and the far-off past gathered around
Cauld House, as the winter began. What are the
neighbours doing in the cellar? Why is it getting
so cold, so very cold? Why are the villagers so
unfriendly? What is happening to Ally Shore? She
seems to be changing – was she ever really a little
girl?

Ally, Ally, Aster is an atmospheric story of magic
forces in the modern world.

Ann Halam is the pen name of author Gwyneth
Jones, who writes science fiction for adults. Ann
Halam's other books in Puffin are *King Death's
Garden* and *The Daymaker*. She is married and
lives in Brighton.

Other books by Ann Halam

THE DAYMAKER
KING DEATH'S GARDEN

Ally, Ally, Aster

Ann Halam

PUFFIN BOOKS

PUFFIN BOOKS

Published by the Penguin Group
27 Wrights Lane, London w8 5tz, England
Viking Penguin Inc., 40 West 23rd Street, New York, New York 10010, USA
Penguin Books Australia Ltd, Ringwood, Victoria, Australia
Penguin Books Canada Ltd, 2801 John Street, Markham, Ontario, Canada l3r 1b4
Penguin Books (NZ) Ltd, 182–190 Wairau Road, Auckland 10, New Zealand

Penguin Books Ltd, Registered Offices: Harmondsworth, Middlesex, England

First published by George Allen & Unwin Ltd 1981
Published in Puffin Books 1990
1 3 5 7 9 10 8 6 4 2

Filmset in Linotron Sabon
by Centracet, Cambridge

Printed and bound in Great Britain by
Cox & Wyman Ltd, Reading

Contents

1   *A Special Little Curio*

It was a wonderful summer day. The hedgerows glowed green under a warm blanket of blue sky. The air was full of sunlight, like a dish of cream.

'I'll have to have a window open,' said Tom Shore.

The windscreen was milky and dripping with condensation; he could barely see. He turned up the collar of his coat and glanced back at his sister.

'Keep your eyes on the road,' she snapped, and gave a twitch. She had been twitching ever since they started out. That was why she was in the back seat. She could not help herself – every so often she jumped and winced, as if something was dragging her. 'No window – it's bad enough as it is.'

Tom groaned, hunched his shoulders and peered, shivering, out ahead at the hot summer landscape.

What was it Edith was holding so tightly? What was it that was fighting in her hands and wriggling furiously to get free? It was not a white mouse, nor a tiny bird with pale fluttering wings. It was alive, but it had no right to be.

'I'll strangle you,' muttered Edith, crushing it viciously in her blue benumbed fingers. But how can you strangle a piece of paper?

'What's up with it anyway?'

'It doesn't like the weather,' said Edith.

The car drew up. They were in the High Street of a pleasant small country town. They crossed the market square, collecting some strange glances for their unseasonable clothes, and marched straight into a shop – an antique shop. Clong! said the mellow bell behind the door.

The shop owner didn't know what to make of this pair. Except for being dressed for the Arctic they looked an ordinary middle-aged couple. They asked questions about a piece of Chelsea that wasn't all it should be, and they offered such bad prices that they must know a lot about the trade. But if they were dealers or collectors surely they would know better than to look so anxious and eager. The woman customer was certainly in a bad way. She kept grinding her teeth; funny blue colour in the face as well. At last it came:

'You were at the Askew auction, I suppose?' said the woman. She was trying to sound casual, but she was shivering all over with excitement.

The shopkeeper tried to think of what she had bought at that sale. Some books, and a box of old toys . . . Maybe there was something rare among those mouldering bales of calf and morocco. She thought she had seen a rather nice china doll in the toy box, but surely that couldn't be worth all this frantic excitement – the woman was shaking like a leaf. Mrs Fisher (the shop owner) immediately decided that she wasn't going to let go of this treasure – whatever it was – very easily. She said, in a bored voice:

'Actually – I haven't touched the things from the Askew's yet. They're still in their boxes. Would you like to look at some mourning rings? Victorian, very nice . . .'

The man and woman looked at each other. Then the woman said rudely, 'Unpack them now. We'll wait. Be quick about it.'

Mrs Fisher began to think she must have a first folio Shakespeare in one of those dusty parcels. *She* didn't

8

look excited though. She began to take out the nice mourning rings:

'Oh, I'm so sorry. But I really couldn't make you wait so long. See how the lock of hair has been worked into the gold filigree.'

'We'll stay over and come back tomorrow.'

'Oh dear. I'm afraid you might be wasting your time.'

'How long?'

'Well, I really couldn't say. Perhaps you should take my card and phone me in a week or so.'

Mrs Fisher was enjoying herself, but goodness! How that woman stared. It was quite frightening.

'Come – we won't quibble. We'll take the lot. Name a price.'

Mrs Fisher was amazed. But she was determined not to give up the unknown prize. Besides, she did not like this woman. There was something funny about her altogether. She got up, saying very firmly. 'I'm *sorry*' – meaning to show this odd couple the door.

She stood up. But the strange woman had begun to behave more strangely than ever. She had one hand up in the air, and she was waving it about. The other was still thrust into the pocket of her sheepskin jacket, twitching as if it had hold of something alive. Suddenly she seemed larger than life. Mrs Fisher felt cold all over. She saw, beyond the bulky brown sheepskin shoulder, the man turning round from a tall grandfather clock on the other side of the room and looking horrified. She heard him shout something – 'Edith! Have you . . .' The loud voice boomed in and out and round about the polished, pretty furniture, the trays of trinkets and alcoves of pictures and shelves of china . . . Mrs Fisher looked down and saw her hand on a doorknob. But it was not the front door of the shop. She was in her back

9

hall, in the act of unlocking her storeroom. She had just a moment of bewilderment, and then she only wondered why anything had seemed strange:

'Well, well. The Askew boxes are in here somewhere. Just you have a good poke round. The customer's always right, as they say.'

'Did you have to hypnotize her?'

'Yes. I know by now when they aren't going to sell. It is all right. She won't remember anything odd. There's nothing for her to remember.'

The front room of Tom and Edith Shore's flat was an uncomfortable place. It was piled high with china dogs as big as doorstops, gilt clocks crowned with cupids, glass cases full of faded butterflies. And then, of course, there was the horrible chill in the air. A bitter draught of winter trickling into the indoor summer warmth. The brother and sister had taken off their coats, and wrapped blankets around them instead. On top of a harpsichord lay the thing they had bought from Mrs Fisher. It seemed to be that china doll the shop owner had glimpsed in her toy box. It was a small thing, with a hard white little face and a floss of pale hair. If it had ever had rosy cheeks and blue eyes the paint must have worn away; there was no trace of colour now.

They had hunted this curiosity painfully, wearily, for months, with a mountain of bric-à-brac gathering round them. They had to keep buying, to ward off the greedy suspicions of people like Mrs Fisher. Tom peered at the thing dubiously, from a safe distance.

'Think of it as a key,' said his sister. 'It is a combination key with two parts. Now we've got both. We fit them together, we take it up there, and we fit it into the lock. That's all there is to it.'

It was Edith who had found the first clue, and had the boldness to take it seriously. The Shores were indeed antique dealers, but quite soon now they were going to say goodbye to shops and sales for ever. They had made their fortunes – if only things worked out.

'Suppose she turns funny?' said Tom.

They both looked at the doll, and then moved away a step or two, putting their heads together as if afraid of being overheard.

'Not likely,' muttered Edith. 'I've adjusted it. She won't know the meaning of – you know – money. Serious money. You'll see what I mean in a minute.'

But it was more than a minute. Edith fetched out the manual she had got out of the library and checked her calculations. Possibly a few hundred years ago an informed person would have been shocked to see such a practical handbook so freely available, but nobody would have thought anything of seeing it in Edith's hands today: just a middle-aged lady's hobby – like macramé. Edith muttered over some bits of Latin, with the help of a dictionary, and perused her tables. She found that they had better wait for moonset. They settled down to a comfortless vigil, hunched in their blankets.

The night grew old. Outside, a tiny cool white moon slipped, unnoticed, out of the city sky. Edith looked at her watch, coughed and reached for her reading glasses. She picked up the thing she had been carrying all day. It was quite limp now.

It was only a page out of a book. It had come from a rather handsome copy of a collection of north country legends. Edith had bought the book from someone who didn't know what an old illustrated volume like that could fetch, and she had noticed something funny about the back pages. It was then that she'd taken her handbook out of the library. Edith had vision, in her way. She wasn't afraid of trying something just because it sounded fantastic. Not when there was 'serious money' at stake.

'Now, you see, I just read this,' she whispered to Tom.

It was an old, old story. It was told in such grand and ancient-sounding language that it seemed to have come out of the white northern mists along with Odin and Thor and the rest of the people of Valhalla. Edith plodded through it, with only the vaguest idea of what it was about.

'The king was grieved, but it was the law of the land that any sickly child must be exposed, even if it was his own first-born. But the queen went to a wisewoman for charms to protect her infant from the cold. Then the little prince Karr was laid out in the snow, and when they came again at dawn (for the law said that if a child lived one night it had proved itself) the baby was gone. "The daughter of the Winter King had taken him" – so people said of all children who were given to the snow . . .'

Edith read about the wisewoman and the queen, and the sorrow of the king. Years passed by. The king and the queen had two other sons, who grew up to be strong men, but hated each other. The king died, the two brothers fought for the crown. Now the first son had not died in the snow. He had been spirited away and had grown up in the magic court of the Winter King, in caverns of ice. When the kingdom was divided he came back, with an ice princess, a daughter of Winter, who would help him claim his throne. She did help him, but heartlessly, so that he killed his own mother and his brothers before he reached his goal. It was then that he found the royal treasure would not bear his hand. Ice was in his blood; he could not touch mortal riches. Without the sacred crown he could not be called lawful sovereign. In his despair Karr swore that there would be no more kings, no more blood shed over possession of the royal treasure. And standing there in the royal treasure chamber he charged the immortal Alvilda, the ice spirit, to guard it so that no one could touch it, for she had promised to give the crown to him, and she must hold it until he could claim it – that is, for ever. Then Alvilda said: 'I will. And the bones of the earth shall crack and break before my promise fails.' That was the end of Karr the king, because he set a blade to his heart when she had spoken. He fell, and his flesh left him, and his body became a pool of icy water on the floor of the chamber. But after that the kingdom dwindled and . . .

Edith put the paper down. She had not read the whole legend. It wasn't necessary. You only had to read little bits. Other parts had different purposes. Had she read enough? The cold was intense. Tom shifted about uneasily.

'I suppose a lot of people used to go after the treasure once,' said Edith. 'So someone thought they'd be clever and break up the combination and hide it. Like two keys to a safety deposit. Well, they were a bit too clever. Stop fidgeting, Tom. There's nothing to be afraid of. You'll see.'

Then something happened. It was either too swift or too strange for eyes to take in, but after it the temperature of the room had risen to an easier level, and standing in front of Tom and Edith there was a white, naked girl. Not a powerful ice sorceress; just a little girl.

13

She was alive. Her eyes, which had no colour, were open.

'You see,' said Edith proudly. 'I worked it out.'

The ice child, in the moment of coming awake, was at once wary and poised, like a guard disturbed. But then she realized something. Her hands dropped to her sides.

'You're not *all here* are you?' said Edith, with gleeful confidence. Everything was as planned.

'No,' said the child. Her voice was thin and flat, like a doll's voice.

'Right,' said Edith. 'But you know where the rest of you is, and so do we. That's where we're all going. I'm your Aunt Edith, and this is your Uncle Tom. When we get where we're going I can put you back together again, if you are a good girl. You won't have to worry about anything any more. Do you understand?'

The little girl, helpless and small, looked at the two adults. For a second something flashed in her colourless eyes — something not helpless and not childlike. But Edith missed that expression. She only saw the face the child showed next, which was perfectly docile and meek.

'Yes, Aunt Edith,' said the creature timidly, in her doll's voice.

'Good. Come on then, I'll get you dressed.'

When they had gone Tom picked up the paper. It seemed to him unchanged — he had never noticed the strange faint markings between the lines that Edith had seen. They were gone now. He shook his head, and went to stick the pages carefully back into the book. It might still fetch something, if a buyer didn't look too closely. He smiled as he read the faded name and address on the fly leaf:

Gertrude Carey
Cauld House
Cauld.

Everything was going very smoothly indeed.

2 *Cauld House Moor*

'I'm sorry Mum, but the fact is, people of thirteen generally prefer to pick their own friends.'

The Pledges had moved house. They had hardly begun to unpack, and all four of them had been quite disgusted to see more removal vans come growling up the rough road from the village, invading their lonely moor. They were to have neighbours. Richard was standing at the window in the front of the Pledges' new living-room, watching an endless series of packing-cases being carried into next door. It had quite spoiled his day, but Mum was already trying to make the best of it. There was a girl, it seemed.

'She'll be going to your school.'

Richard shook his head (these people certainly had plenty of furniture). 'Look,' he said firmly, 'if the Fates mean me to get to know the young lady it will happen. I don't believe in interfering with destiny.'

'Don't be so pompous,' said his mother. 'Come and help me count these curtain hooks.'

But Richard murmured something vague and slipped out of the room.

Richard and Laura's parents had been trying to move out of the city for years. But all the houses were horrible, said Dad. He hated the dreary raw estates in the suburbs. He wanted to live somewhere real. Richard and Laura got used to a restless feeling of being between houses, which seemed to become permanent. Then they heard of Cauld House. 'An amazing piece of luck,' said Dad. Mum said, teasing him, that it was not luck, it was a sinister plot. What happened was that Mr and Mrs Pledge were invited to view half an old farmhouse, up on the moor outside a place called Cauld. The invitation came from a firm of estate agents they'd never heard of. They went to see, out of curiosity, and found the place sound, modernized, perfect in every way. The terms were very reasonable too. Mr Thorhall, the agent, explained that they were under a special agreement with the owner not to let the property unless they could let it complete, and there was another couple wanting 'Number Three' – the other half of the house. Here was the sinister part: Mum, who didn't like the hint of an eccentric owner somewhere, tried to write to this person. She found there was no owner at all. It was just a property company. And they'd never heard of Thorhall and Thorhall's 'special agreement'.

'Oh, it's quite simple,' said Dad. 'Estate agents tell each other about their clients, I suppose. Thorhall's heard of us, they had half a house on their hands, and the rest is just sales talk or something. In any case, let's not quarrel with it. It's my ancestral home!'

It was his 'ancestral home' because his wife and children had been groaning for months that he wouldn't be satisfied with anything less than battlements and a deer park. But it was also true, in a way. 'My great-grandfather came from round here. I'm sure it was Cauld. Yes, I can remember my grandad talking about it. It's a really bitter place for winter weather. Snow and ice guaranteed. It is something to do with exposure to the north.'

'Thanks,' said Richard. '*Now* you tell us.'

Having escaped from the curtains, Richard got out of the house as well. There was a garden with a thick, prickly hedge dividing it from Number Three. It was a

17

blue August morning, the air was still sharp, but it would be a warm day. He could hear voices around the corner of the house. He looked and saw his sister Laura on a stepladder doing something to a gutter, with Dad prancing underneath, calling directions. They seemed to be enjoying themselves, so he decided to leave them in peace. He sat by the garden gate to inspect his new home. It was a thick grey stone building, unevenly divided into two parts. The Pledges had the front door, with a deep porch and '1596' carved into the stone gable. There was a motto too. 'QUIS CUSTODIET . . .' read Richard. The rest was indistinct, but he could guess what it must be. He knew the Latin tag which asks: 'Who will guard the guards themselves?' But what is there to 'guard' up here? he wondered. Number Three had had to have all their huge packing-cases carted round behind the building, because their door was the natural door of a working farmhouse, in the yard at the back. Their front garden was full of scraps, straw and newspapers, and some smaller boxes that hadn't been taken in yet. There was no one in sight just at the moment. Richard casually leaned over the bramble barrier. But all he got for his curiosity was prickled – and the strange information that the new neighbours owned fifteen or twenty rather fancy old clocks. How odd! He wondered whether they were as displeased as the Pledges at finding they had to share Cauld House right from the start.

'I suppose we both thought the other people might not turn up for a good while, knowing how long arranging to move usually takes. It's those estate agents' fault. I'll have to keep young Laura under control,' he thought. She had already been muttering about having stupid people breathing down your neck, when you'd just moved to somewhere lonely and exciting. The little idiot would be dressing up as a ghost and trying to scare the neighbours off, or some such ridiculous trick, if he didn't watch out.

Someone shouted from the back of Number One. They might have shouted 'Richard!' He quickly slid his legs over the wall and made off down the road. There was not another building in sight. There wasn't even a tree or a bush. A trickle of rough road went down the hill to Cauld in one direction, and in the other away to nowhere, to somewhere in Yorkshire. If you walked to the end of the ridge you could see a great vista of reservoirs and plantations falling away to the south. The big chemical plant were Mum worked was a busy smudge in one corner. To the north there was nothing but whaleback on whaleback of purple and brown. No mountains, no valleys, no farmland, no towns. They might as well have been living on the edge of an ocean. And Cauld itself, he already knew, was just a street, with a pub and a shop and a small station and an *enormous* station-yard full of heaps of coke and coal. 'Hasn't diesel and electric reached this line yet?' he asked Mum sarcastically, when they were visiting Cauld, before the move. 'That's not for the trains,' she said. 'That's for the winter, when the village gets cut off. Oh yes – it happens regularly.' They pulled faces at each other. They did not appreciate the romance of such trials the way Laura and Dad did. Remembering that day, Richard suddenly grinned to himself as he walked along. Dad had tried to tell the Cauldians about the great-grandfather, and the ancestral connections, and he'd certainly got the *Cauld* shoulder. 'Pledge? Oh no. No one of that name here. Never had any . . .' Poor Dad. He just did not have the most reliable memory.

Richard was a good way out on the ridge now, and the house was out of sight behind a heaving up of one of those purple waves. He might have been on the wrong side of the moon. Well, it's certainly peaceful, he admitted. He turned off the road on to what seemed to be a path, and followed it through the heather until it died. The ridge was flat on top, but not so hard and bony as it looked. Away from the road the ground broke up – there was a big concave patch which was green instead of heathery, rustling with white tails of bog cotton, and looking strangely purposeful, like a stage or an arena. There were bits of walls, or what looked like walls, scattered on it, and ditches cutting into it. Canals, said Richard to himself, on the face of Mars. His track had disappeared quite close to a tumbled sort of shelter of boulders. The late summer sky was perfectly blue and a lark was singing high overhead. Richard sat down, rested his back against the stones and gradually slipped away into a dream of sun and quiet.

He was thinking about the girl next door. He had not seen her. He wondered whether she would be all right. In spite of his protests, he did realize that if she was coming to his school and travelling on the same train every day he would probably have to get to know her.

'It all turns on how old she is . . .' Mum had said an odd thing about that.

'Well, how old *is* she? Did you ask?' Richard had inquired.

'Yes, I did,' said Mum. 'But they didn't know.'

'What on earth do you mean?'

'What I said. I asked the man – her uncle – and he said, "Er – twelve, I think." That's *exactly* what he said. Then the woman said, "Thirteen." I mean, she butted in. Then they both glared at each other. I changed the subject. Then the girl appeared, and I could see what they meant. One of those wispy things; small enough to be about ten, until you take a good look. Then you realize . . . ' Mum was frowning at her memory of the strange girl.

Richard said, 'A 45-year-old midget, obviously. Really Mum – the truth is, you ask too many questions and people get bored with answering them straight.'

But it wasn't so. The Shores wanted to be friends. They wanted to be 'Edith and Tom'. They were very keen on little niece Alice getting to know Richard and Laura. She'd had a lonely life, she needed to be taken out of herself . . .

'No – that's one thing she doesn't need!' said one or other of the Shores, and they both chuckled. It was true that Mum had been out on the doorstep chatting for a good half-hour last night, getting all this gossip, so you couldn't say she'd been chased off. Mum gave her verdict: Edith and Tom were a little odd, but you ought to try and get on with your neighbours. Moreover, the little girl deserved a chance. 'There's something sad there,' said Mum. 'Where are her parents for instance? You should at least try to be nice to her.'

People prefer to choose their own friends . . .

Richard sat up sharply. He had not been asleep, or even dozing, but time seemed to have passed without his noticing. The light had changed completely. The sky wasn't blue any more. For a moment he thought he'd done a Rip van Winkle trick, and lost a day, but he looked at his watch and it was still morning. But everything was grey, and the stone at his back was cold as ice. Now how on earth did it change so fast? he wondered. He began to get up, but then he held himself still. The lark which had been singing was right in front of him, perching on a lichened stone. He could see the curling feathers raised along the back of its head; it ducked and slicked its neat bill against the stone. Richard stayed half on his knees, watching with delight. The lark briskly tidied a feather or two and looked up again, its small head poised with a very alert and intelligent look of attention. It was watching something too. Something Richard couldn't see.

Then he heard voices. He jumped. *But the lark didn't.* Two voices – one clear and sharp, one more a sort of mutter. It was a quarrel. He thought it had been going on for a while, but only just got loud enough to be heard. Richard knelt, fascinated, watching the lark that did not stir, that sat and observed with interest a quarrel between two human beings. Is it tame? he wondered. Maybe it's going to go over and tell them to shut up. Maybe I'm dreaming. Cautiously he eased around until he could peer over the boulders. He didn't see much. The mist that obscured the blue sky seemed to be building up on the ground too, in the swift way moorland mist can. Just as he got his eyes above the stone there came a sharp unmistakable sound – Crack! A slap. Someone had just turned on their heel and was marching away. It was a girl – small, in blue jeans, with very pale hair. The other half of the quarrel, he couldn't quite make out. It was crouched down on the ground; he had the impression of something brown, and big eyes, and then it had scampered away. It seemed to be sobbing or whimpering. It moved very low on the ground.

Richard turned round again. He sat down. The lark

saw that human movement and at once, with a flirt of wings, was away in the air.

'What on earth have I just seen?' thought Richard. Someone being told off. And refusing to go. And getting slapped and running away, crying. Little Alice Shore has a pet (it *could* have been a dog). She brings it out on the moor, she's a bit childish – she makes up a voice for doggy, and has a make-believe quarrel with him . . .

It was very quiet, now that the lark had gone. Richard felt he didn't particularly want to meet the girl next door just now. He thought she might not like to know anyone had eavesdropped on her let's-pretend games. He sat on where he was for a good five minutes, giving her time to get away. The August sun had lost all its heat, the bare green place with its Martian canals had a dismal uncanny look under the grey veiled sky. When at last he thought it was safe to get up, and started off for the road again, he was amazed at how cold he felt. It was as if August had been invaded by winter, just here on this little patch of moor.

He saw the man on the bicycle from quite a way off, and was glad to know exactly where the road lay, in this purple sea of heather. But he was surprised to find the man waiting for him when he reached the verge. He was in uniform. He leaned on the handlebars of his bike and said, after a long slow stare:

'So. You're back.'

'I'm sorry. Were you waiting for me? Was I trespassing? Aren't we allowed on the moor?'

'Oh no,' said the man. 'You're all right out there so long as he's about. If he is a bit windy. Did you see them meeting?'

Windy? The day was perfectly still.

'Scared – you know.'

23

Richard thought this must be the village idiot. He said, trying to be polite, 'I saw a sort of mist.' Perhaps this odd chap was talking about hot and cold air meeting, something like what Dad had mentioned. 'Well – I must be off.'

But the postman, or whatever he was, wouldn't let Richard on his way before they had had a strange rambling chat – about how Richard had *every right* to be on the moor, but the house now, the house was another question . . .

Laura was sitting on the garden wall, making currant-leaf transfers on the back of her hand.

'I saw you,' she said. 'You've been on the moor, you lazy pig. What were you talking to the stationmaster about?'

'Was that the stationmaster? I thought it was the postman. He's mad anyway.'

He told her about the odd conversation. Laura began to laugh. 'Oh Richard, you've got it all upside down. He means people have always lived on the moor, but this house is "new". He thinks 1596 is modern. He's been telling me all about it. There's a Viking village.'

'You mean Saxon, I expect.'

'No, it's true. They lived here before William the Conqueror.'

They went indoors. Richard had to face the curtain hooks, and a hundred other tasks of unpacking and setting up. Dad said Laura could be right about the Vikings, and anyway a local man would know. Nice of him to come up and say hello.

'Is that what he came for?' thought Richard. 'I wonder.' It had felt more like a warning than a welcome.

*

Laura and Richard were picking gooseberries. It was the day after Richard's walk on the moor, and the chilly patch he'd found there seemed to have spread itself. The sun had not appeared at all, and they were wearing thick jumpers as they scrambled around the prickly hedge. Laura was telling Richard more of what the stationmaster had said: 'There was a family called Carey, you see, and they lived up here until they all died out. They wouldn't let anyone else near the place. I asked him why anyone would *want* to come near the place, and he just looked sly. I think the Careys must have been a gang, like in a Western, and this was their hideout. He said the moor was haunted until the Careys left. That proves it, doesn't it? I mean that's just the sort of story robbers would tell to keep people away. I bet that's why the people in Cauld are so unfriendly. They think we're going to be robbers too.'

'That's funny,' said Richard, falling in with her romancing, 'because when I read the motto over the door, I thought the people here must have been some kind of policemen. Have you seen it?'

But Laura wasn't interested in 'Who guards the guards?' She had a romance much nearer to hand than long-dead cops and robbers. She was now peering through the hedge at the front of Number Three, with a glint in her eye that he didn't like.

'Laur! You're on their side of the hedge.'

'Oh! How can you tell?' said Laura. 'Anyway, they want us to be friends.' She continued wriggling. 'At least that's their story. How can we be friends if we never meet her?'

He knew exactly what was going on in his sister's head. The little girl – Ally, her aunt called her – must be a prisoner, a kidnapped heiress, a slave chained up scrubbing floors, a ballerina or a gymnast being forced to do something wicked, like cheat at the Olympic Games, by her cruel guardians. He got hold of the back of her jumper and hung on.

'No you don't!'

'I'm not doing anything.'

'Oh Laur, just think what an idiot you'll feel if you creep up and peer in the window and somebody catches you.'

Laura tried to pull away from him. 'You never want anything to happen!' she protested. 'You just want to sit around and keep out of things.'

'Ssh, ssh.'

But it was too late. Laura was yelling at the top of her voice, and the aunt popped out of the front door of Number Three. It was very embarrassing. She was just an ordinary middle-aged lady, rather fat. She came trotting over to where he and Laura were wrestling and snarling and said, in the bright, stupid voice adults use on strange children.

'Are you picking the nice gooseberries, then?'

'No,' thought Richard. 'We are having a fight.' But the woman seemed to mean well so he just nodded and smiled.

'Have as many as you like,' she said. 'We don't mind. We'd like to see you in our garden.'

'Thank you very much,' said Richard politely.

'Yes,' she said. 'Any time you like. You may want to come over here a lot. I mean, when your mummy and daddy are back at work. You won't like being alone in the house I expect.'

'Well, thank you,' said Richard. 'But . . .' He began to explain: Dad would be home the same time as them most days. He taught music at a special school that was out on the healthy moor quite close to Cauld. It was a new job. Dad was going to enjoy it much more than working in hospitals in the city. Richard was quite happy to explain it all to their neighbour. He thought it was kind of her to make the offer. But Laura, who had stopped wriggling, said suddenly, loudly:

'I'm going in. Come on, Richard.'

He hadn't a chance to make her behave. She just marched off. Luckily the woman didn't seem to notice how rude Laura had been. She gave another false bright smile and went back to her house. Richard hurried after Laura.

'What's got into you? Why were you so rude?'

Laura was sitting at the kitchen table, the tin bowl of gooseberries flung down anyhow, spilling its red and golden globes across the scrubbed wood. She was looking rebellious.

'What's got into *you*?' she demanded. 'Telling her all that. It's none of her business. Couldn't you see what she was getting at? Hinting Mum and Dad shouldn't leave us alone. Trying to lure us into their house. Hinting something nasty about our house too. Don't you get it?'

She was off on another of her flights of fancy. Richard resignedly began to calm her down, telling her she mustn't go making up incredible stories about ordinary people. Laura did not tell Richard about the other thing. The way Edith Shore started *moving her hands*. He hadn't noticed, and he'd just think she was making it up. She let him talk on, and picked up one of the gooseberries. It was a fine fat specimen, but there was something wrong with it. The rich reddish colour was blotched, as if it was frost-bitten.

'That's funny!'

She showed it to Richard. She was sure, in her own mind, she knew which side of the hedge this berry had come from. Most of the berries were unmarred. Most of them came from the Pledges' side of the garden.

'Must be a freak cold spot,' said Richard. 'I've heard of them.'

'Yes, I've heard of them too,' muttered Laura under her breath. 'You get them in haunted houses.'

Edith went back into Number Three. She went through to the front of the house, where they had had to make one room their own, and Tom was crouched over a big fire. She peeled away a couple of cardigans, and sat down.

'Saw them off?' said Tom.

'Nothing of the kind,' said Edith impatiently. 'We've got to be subtle. Don't worry: they will be scared. They will be haunted. I got some information out of the boy, I know which evenings will be best for us. But we don't want them to suspect their nice kind neighbours.'

'Oh, I get you,' said Tom morosely. He was dismal at finding they had neighbours at all. It seemed to him the plan was going wrong in more ways than one. But Edith said it was just a minor setback. She had her manual, and soon she would send the Pledges packing. Shadows in the garden, faces at the windows, strange whisperings at night.

'The children will be easier to deal with, but the parents will feel it too. Besides, we've got our cover.' She nodded at the pile of boxes that filled half this room. 'And, besides, it is good for you-know-who to see the children playing about. I don't think we'll really let her play with them. We don't want her getting close to anyone, not right on our doorstep.'

'That's another thing,' said Tom, looking worried again. 'I've been meaning to ask. Are you sure?'

'Sure?'

'That she'll do it, I mean.'

The creature might be anywhere. She was so uncomfortable to live with at the moment that they couldn't keep their eyes on her much of the time. Tom looked over his shoulder at the closed door, and Edith lowered her voice as she answered:

'Listen. They *buried* their treasure, you know. Barrows – heaps of stone. Or chambers deep in the earth. Think of it – a thousand years. That's a *very* long time, shut up in a stone safe. I don't say I know exactly what goes on in the head of a thing like that, but consider this: A part of her is still there now. She can make the comparison. Oh, yes, she made a promise. But to whom? Who cares, after all this time? No, no, don't worry. She'll do what we want her to do. And then, you know we don't have to . . .' Edith's voice sank to a muttering.

She need not have worried. Ally was not listening at the keyhole. She was sitting at an upstairs window overlooking the moor. A big spider had her web there, and Ally had just delicately, tenderly, freed a peacock butterfly from the cruel trap. She got up, opened the window, tossed the butterfly out into the free air and stood there for a moment with her arms outstretched, her face to the sky. But the butterfly fell. It landed on the garden path. All the rich colour had gone from its wings in the brief moment when Ally held it in her hand, and its bold markings were now traced in white on silver. It was a flower of ice and snow, but it was dead.

'How long are we going to have to put up with *this*

anyway?' said Tom, down below. He wasn't talking about the Pledges.

'Oh, that's all right. Only another two days to the turn.'

This was the end of August, and the moon was nearly full.

3   Rather a Cool Customer

The road from Cauld House into Cauld was a steep and winding hill. A little way below the house a stone bridge carried it over a narrow dry valley, and right at the foot of the hill was Cauld station. Laura and Richard felt like gunslingers taking over a town whenever they walked around the station yard and started to climb again, up the steep blackened street of stone houses. Everybody seemed to be hurrying out of their way. Mr Midfirth the stationmaster said the Cauld people would 'see the Pledges through a winter' before they made friends. But at least he was friendly, and always ready to chat, especially to Laura. Richard heard some amazing things from his sister, all beginning: 'Mr Midfirth says . . .' There were ghosts and goblins and buried treasures under every boulder on the moor, it seemed. However, when Richard himself asked about that arena with the Martian canals the stationmaster said, sensibly enough, that it was just old sheep pens. And when he mentioned Vikings 'before William the Conqueror' Mr Midfirth just laughed and said, 'Eh, lad. Do I look as old as all that?' Obviously Laura was considered a much better audience for tall stories.

It turned out that the Pledges and the Shores weren't likely to be friends. Richard made excuses about going next door, in case Laura should do or say something stupid. The offers were not repeated. Besides, Mum said that Edith Shore spent too much of her time asking

what you'd paid for things, and picking up the orna-
ments and sniffing at them disparagingly. 'It's probably
for the best. We're close enough without being in and
out of each other's houses all day.' Richard and Laura
agreed. Except that sometimes it would have been nice
to think there was friendly company next door. Sometimes, if you were by yourself, Number One could seem
a lonely place. The quiet of the moor was strange after
the city, and in the evening long, peculiar shadows
stretched through the rooms of the old house.

As the weather got better, in the last days of the
holidays, Richard and Laura went out on the moor a
good deal. A couple of times Richard noticed a figure
that must be Ally, but whenever he saw that small pale
head he led Laura another way. He knew this was
unfriendly, but he didn't like the idea of interrupting
any more odd games. As far as he could work out the
Shores did not have a dog. No pets at all.

Someone had made a mistake about Ally. Richard
looked for her on his first day back at the Sir David
Morrison Comprehensive High School – Morrison, for
short. But she wasn't there. She turned up on the second
day of term, with the rest of the new first years. He saw
one of the senior girls pinning up lists of the new classes
and read: Alice Shore.

'That's a mistake,' he said.

'Mind your own business,' said the girl.

'But it is. She lives next door to me. She's my age. She
doesn't belong in first year.'

The senior listened to him and said, 'Maybe she's a
year behind. Maybe she's been ill. What's the name
again?'

'Alice Shore.'

The senior had been marching little boys and girls about all morning. *Some* of them might have passed for thirteen, but others looked . . . She stared at Richard, decided it must be some feeble joke, and went off without answering.

In the afternoon there was a lower school assembly, to start the year, and Richard saw Ally in her line. He was amazed. There was no mistaking that fluffy whitish hair, but he was sure he had seen someone not only actually bigger, but also a lot more substantial. He remembered his mother saying 'a wisp of a thing'. I must have got the wrong impression, he thought. After all, there was a mist.

Ally didn't take the train from Cauld. On consideration, Edith and Tom had decided it would be safer to drive her in and out. So Richard did not have to meet her. Mum asked him how she was getting on. Was he being nice to her? Richard made reasonable excuses. After a few days, though, he had to admit to himself that he was definitely avoiding little Ally. And it wasn't just because in school you don't mix with younger kids. He couldn't tell exactly *why* it was. He just 'didn't like the look of her'.

Morrison Comprehensive High School was a big place. It had once been two schools, a girls' grammar and a boys' technical school. The campuses had flowed into one. All the changes were over now, but there were still a few relics of the past. One of these was the senior mistress, a tall thin lady with a greenish old gown perpetually falling off her shoulders, gold-rimmed half-glasses perched on her nose, and a deceptive air of absent-mindedness. She was the chief authority in West Building, where Richard spent most of his life – as did

Ally Shore. Richard was on good terms with Dr Radleigh. She ran the school chess club. When he saw her sailing down the corridor at him, at lunchtime on the Friday of the first week of term, he did not panic. He thought it was about chess.

'Ah, Richard,' said Dr Radleigh. 'A word.'

Her hand fastened on his arm – she had this way of gripping you, like an eagle's claw – and to his surprise she started to lead him away. Without speaking she kept him under arrest like this until they got to the West Building canteen. Richard was bewildered. They stood at the glass door. Dr Radleigh was peering inside. What was she looking at?

'I hear your family has moved,' she said quietly. 'To the Cauld House Moor. An interesting spot.'

'Yes. That's right.' He was trying to work out what crime of his could be punished by making him look at first years eating their dinner.

'Mmm. I must refresh my memory about Cauld House. You have neighbours, also new to the area? And they have sent a child to this school?'

'Yes, that's right,' said Richard again. He had just realized what she was looking at. It was the table where Alice Shore was sitting. She was at the head of it. Ten other little girls had left two seats empty, one on either side of her. They were sitting with their hands folded, quiet and still in the babble of the canteen. 'They are waiting for her to finish her meal,' said Dr Radleigh. As she spoke, one of the children got up, picked up the water jug and went, politely, to refill Ally's glass.

'What beautiful manners,' said the senior mistress. 'Your friend seems to exert a powerful influence, Richard.'

'She's not – ' he began, but Dr Radleigh was still speaking.

'Richard,' she said. 'I notice there's something missing from the young lady's table. Will you please go and offer her the salt?'

Mystified, Richard walked into the canteen. He felt a complete fool. The duty teachers were obviously wondering what he was up to. Still, he went and found a salt shaker and took it over. He held it out. The little girl lifted up her pale face and looked at him coolly, and looked at the salt.

'Er – thought you might want?' he muttered, embarrassed.

'Who told you to do that?' said Ally. Then she looked over his shoulder and saw Dr Radleigh watching. She laughed, took the shaker from Richard and tipped salt on to her palm. It lay there, the grains no whiter than her skin. Still looking over Richard's shoulder, she put the handful in her mouth. Then she gave him back the shaker. She didn't seem to be at all uncomfortable, she didn't even grab for her water glass. Only, she began to look surprised that her *servant* hadn't gone away. Richard went. When he got to the door of the canteen again, red in the face and very confused, Dr Radleigh had gone.

Richard climbed the hill from Cauld, slowly. His umbrella was held down low, his collar was up, and a wool hat was pulled over his ears, but the rain still managed to get to him. He was late. He had stayed clearing up after a drama class, and missed his usual train. As he toiled through the wet gloom he was thinking of an odd sight he'd seen, from the drama-room window at four o'clock. A crowd of people milled

35

around the school gates, waiting for buses. You could wait in the bike sheds, but they were inside the walls. If you wanted to make a good rush at your bus you had to be outside, and there was only one little shelter. The rain had begun. Richard, looking out of the window, saw Ally Shore standing in the shelter, all alone, waiting for Edith or Tom to pick her up. The crowd was mostly kids: they always got out first. But that didn't explain Ally's splendid isolation – they wouldn't let any teacher or even any seniors stay dry while they got wet, would they? It was most odd.

Richard's trousers were flapping wetly. He brooded on the state they would be in, and pondered on a pair of wellington boots. Horrible, ugly things, wellington boots. Perhaps he could keep them in a locker at the station. He was trying to picture Cauld station, and see if there were lockers, when he found he was being watched. It was a very strange sensation. The rain pelted, the wind tussled with his umbrella; there couldn't possibly be anyone about, but the feeling was too strong to ignore. Someone was watching him. He peered ahead and saw that the road was not empty after all. He had got further than he'd known, tramping head down and noticing nothing but his wet feet. There was a bulky black thing – it was Cauld House.

'Is it darker than I thought?'

He looked again. The house stood as normal, grey and grizzled inside its streaming garden. My eyes playing tricks, said Richard to himself. But the moment he started to walk the house was watching him again. Was it the house itself, or was it someone standing by the gate, a threatening shadow ready to grab him as he went inside? The impression was so strong that Richard considered seriously if he might be seeing a real ghost.

He thought of hints of Mr Midfirth's stories, that he had heard from Laura. The ghost on the moor was some kind of 'White Lady' he seemed to remember. Did she do any harm? 'Only to bad people,' said Laura. 'Anyway, she's been gone for years and years.' That sounded like an old man telling scary stories and then regretting it.

'Can't stand here all night,' muttered Richard, and marched forward. With an effort, he made himself pass through the gate, but as he did so he could have *sworn* something malicious and shadowy slipped from behind the currant bush.

'Hey!' cried Richard.

He couldn't help himself, he went splashing after it. 'It' disappeared. Of course 'it' had never existed. Richard found himself ankle deep in the neglected lawn, with his umbrella half inside out. The house stared at him innocently with its drawn curtains and ordinary, homely light shining around them. 'Absurd!' Richard felt annoyed and confused, and very wet. He was not really frightened, he did not really think he had seen a ghost. But he had been made very uncomfortable, and in his mind was planted the seed of a secret dislike for Cauld House, especially in darkness and bad weather. It was a start – just the effect promised by Edith's manual.

When Richard went into the house he found Laura sitting in a blaze of lights. As he opened the front door – it opened straight into the living-room, as is common in old northern houses – she started, and then quickly pushed out of sight something that had been lying by her hand. Richard had a look under that cushion afterwards, and found the poker.

It was that weekend that Mum and Dad suddenly put

a ban on exploring Cauld House Moor. At least, the children were not to go far from the road, and never alone. 'I've been talking to the Shores,' said Dad. 'They reminded me – it's got quite a bad reputation, this piece of country. There's supposed to be an underground river; at any rate there are pot-holes and loose rocks. Too many people have come to grief out there.'

'So be sensible,' said Mum, 'and keep off.'

Laura began to say that the people who had come to grief hadn't fallen in holes through carelessness – not at all. But she remembered that it wasn't the sort of thing Mum and Dad and Richard would listen to. She just muttered that Mr Midfirth said the moor was safe.

Mum and Dad said that these local people weren't always very reliable. Sometimes they talked a lot of nonsense. They had been discussing it with Tom and Edith.

September went on. All four of the Pledges felt – nothing too alarming, just rather uneasy about their new home. It was such a lonely place, and the moors themselves didn't seem so beautiful when you heard they were so treacherous. It was very chilly already, up on the ridge, and perhaps because of the strange stillness they were none of them sleeping very well.

Richard rather forget about Ally Shore. He was keeping out of Dr Radleigh's way anyway, because he felt guilty about the chess club. He had stopped going: it was so late and dark walking up the hill if you stayed after school. But once it happened again. He interrupted one of Ally's games. He was wandering about the playing fields by himself, thinking of nothing in particular, when he heard voices from the shrubbery. It was a curious sound, like several people singing in whispers.

The words did not seem to be English. He quietly went closer, to see what was going on.

In the middle of the bushes there was a little gloomy clearing of bare earth, under a small tree. There was a group of girls who looked like first years, and one among them — who looked different. Richard watched through the leaves for half a minute, then he turned and walked quickly away. He didn't want to know anything about it. But his curiosity was too much for him. Later, he went back and looked again. There was a body hanging from the tree. It was only a sparrow. Probably it had been dead already, and he had only imagined that he saw it fluttering before Ally touched it. Probably he had only seen some peculiar little 'doll's funeral'. Perhaps so. When he reached out to take down the bird he gasped, and pulled his fingers back. Its dead feathers were so cold they had burned him.

4 The Disadvantages of an Ancestral Home

There were a few days of cold weather that put crackling hoar-frost on the grass in Morrison School playing fields. It was unusual for the time of year, and people talked about it. One or two teachers wondered why this cold snap wasn't mentioned in the local weather reports. But the frost soon faded again, and was forgotten. Dr Radleigh said nothing more to Richard, and he was glad to leave well enough alone. Ally Shore seemed to settle down. Other first years continued to have a strange respect for her, but that was all. Except that her games teacher wondered why he couldn't seem to fit Ally into any group. He couldn't seem to make his mind up how tall or how strong she was, from week to week.

At Cauld House the Pledges saw very little of their neighbours, and life went on fairly smoothly. On one evening soon after the early frost had been and gone Laura got into trouble about a dinner plate. It was all right that she had broken it, but *why* had she tried to hide it? She made a big fuss, and denied everything, which was not like Laura. Even after the storm was over she went around saying tragically 'You don't *understand*'. Though what there was to understand about a broken plate, none of her family could work out.

One morning Richard got up very early and found his mother already in the kitchen. She was putting down a saucer of milk at the back door. When he asked her what it was for she said she was feeding the stray cat. She kept seeing a sad-looking little animal hanging around the garden.

'A sort of brown thing?' said Richard. 'Oh. I think I saw it once. Out on the moor. So it's a cat!'

'My, you sound relieved. What did you think it was? The Hound of the Baskervilles? I've never seen it clearly, but I'm sure it's just a stray mog.'

They began to make breakfast. Mum pottered about, putting crockery on the table. Richard laid bacon rashers carefully, fat to lean, in the big frying pan. They talked about Laur.

'It's not like her,' Mum said, 'to try and wriggle out of trouble. And she's too old to believe in fairies.'

'Or ghosts.'

He said it quite cheerfully, but at once he broke off, and there was a strange little silence. Richard felt himself shiver, and suddenly he wondered if his mother had had bad dreams too, or had thought there was something listening at her door, or any other of those ideas that seemed to lie in wait in the shadows, in this house.

'Richard – ' said Mum, in rather an odd voice.

But just at that moment there was a growl and a rumble outside in the road. They were both relieved at the interruption and hurried to the front door. But it wasn't the postman's van after all. It was a larger vehicle, drawing up outside Number Three. On its side was painted the name of a firm and the words 'Building Contractors'. A man got out and went round the back of the Shores' house.

'I wonder what that's about,' said Mum worriedly.

They soon found out. Tom and Edith Shore were going to open an antique shop. They were going to have the blank front of their house altered into a shopfront. Tom was quite happy to tell the neighbours all about it. The alterations wouldn't take long. Only a couple of months . . . or so. The Pledges were horrified.

'This house gets worse and worse!' said Mum.

Dad went to the estate agents after school and was told that it was all above board, all settled, and there was nothing to be done. 'They just seemed to think it was none of their business. I said we weren't going to put up with it and she said – it was the mother, Mrs Thorhall – that if I wanted to put a stop to the Shores I could try, but I had no right to involve them, the agents. That doesn't make sense!'

The Pledges were sitting together in their front room, listening to the bangs beyond the wall. The Shores seemed to have found a very obliging set of builders. 'Are they going to go on all night?'

'Why did the Shores never mention this when they were being so friendly, at the start?'

'Two-faced.'

'Hush, Laura. That sort of talk won't help.'

The banging went on. The Pledges sat close around the fireplace, where they had some logs burning, but a chilly draught had crept under the front door, and was fingering all their spines.

'We'll be sitting here in blankets in a month or so,' said Richard. 'Blankets and earplugs.'

It was an unpleasant prospect.

That Saturday morning Richard went in to Cauld, to buy some eggs and biscuits and things at the supermarket. He had an odd experience there. A man *spoke* to him. All he said was 'How're you getting on on the moor, lad?' As soon as he'd said it the queue at the cash desk were all scowling, and one woman made a remark about the weather. '*Chilly*, isn't it?' she said – obviously and pointedly not talking to Richard. That was the end of that. The Pledges' probation wasn't over yet, it seemed.

'I wonder if we'll last out,' he wondered, tramping up the hill again. Perhaps they wouldn't, in the face of the builders next door on top of everything else. He thought about 'everything else'. There was no getting away from it, 'everything else' added up to the fact that he, Richard, was now afraid of the dark in that house. He had nightmares like a baby. What's more, he was sure the others were suffering too. Perhaps city people just can't get used to an isolated place like this. What a shame.

Then he remembered that Laura was alone up there, because Dad had a staff meeting. In spite of being certain it was all imagination he began to walk faster. When he came to the brow of the hill he was dismayed to see her out by the roadside, sitting on the wall and shivering. The tarpaulin that now covered the front of Number Three flapped emptily – it couldn't be the noise of the builders that had driven her out.

'Laura, what's the matter?'

Laura said, 'Don't worry. It's not *that*.' They looked at each other, and neither cared to explain what 'that' might be. Laura went on, 'It's only Mrs Garth. Her sister was sick on Friday, so she's cleaning today. I was under her feet.'

'Well, d'you think the coast's clear now? It's pretty cold out here.'

The coast was clear. Upstairs the hoover growled and a cracked soprano voice warbled over it. On the kitchen table was a shopping bag, a pair of gloves and a bunch of keys. The keys were labelled 'Cauld House 1'. Mrs

Garth had been caretaker for Thorhalls before the house was let.

'Hey!' said Richard.

In the corner of the Pledges' kitchen there was a door which they had never opened because there was no key. The agents had vaguely promised to find a spare, but they never did. It was obviously a cellar door. A few weeks earlier the children would have been quite excited at the prospect of getting into that cellar. Just now, they had not much enthusiasm for exploring the old house, but a cellar is still a cellar, and a long-locked one could be full of very interesting things.

Richard and Laura saw at once which was the right key. It was huge, black and rusty. It turned, though. The door opened inwards, and they were standing at the top of some wooden steps. Damp, underground air fanned up to them. Laura found a light switch, and the cellar sprang into existence under a single dangling bulb. It was completely empty. One of the walls was obviously a partition, put up when the house was divided and modernized. The floor was of grey, gleaming flagstones. There was nothing at all in the room, not even a pile of old newspapers.

'There's something funny about this,' said Richard. But he could not think what it was. He was about to shut the door again, because there just wasn't anything there, when Laura suddenly cried:

'The door! Look! There's a door in the wall!'

She bounded down the steps and stopped in front of a blank barrier of stone.

'There was a door.'

Richard came and looked. 'It must have been some trick of the shadows,' he told her. But ancient, secret, underground chambers – and the cellar was certainly

44

old – deserve some attention, so they tapped and prised at the craggy stones and the blank pavement for a while, until an exclamation from behind made them both jump. It was Mrs Garth. She hustled them up the steps again, seeming quite angry for some reason. She locked the door as if she was locking up a wild animal.

'We were only having a look,' said Laura. 'It is our cellar.'

Mrs Garth said, 'Don't you ever go down there again. I wouldn't go down there for all the treasure in the world. I nearly had a heart attack when I saw that door open.'

'What treasure?' said Richard.

Mrs Garth looked for a moment as if she had given away a secret, but then she said, 'Oh, you must have heard of the Viking treasure from someone by now. Who'd keep it from you?' She began to tell some tale about gold and jewels hidden on the moor, which obviously was not news to Laura. But when Richard tried to find out what was frightening about treasure, and what was the connection with the Pledges' cellar, she began to flurry about, in a great hurry to finish her work and go.

'Now you remember to tell your mother I never broke that jug. It was on the floor when I came in.'

The jug was a large and handsome one, for flowers. It was lying in pieces on a newspaper on the table. Richard said nothing. As if in protest at the disturbance next door, things had started 'turning up broken' in the Pledges' kitchen. Mrs Garth's name had been mentioned, and the incident of the dinner plate was now seen in a different light. He avoided Laura's eye.

'*Well!*' said Mrs Garth indignantly, seeing his dubious face. She was putting on her coat. 'I don't know. It's

45

not my fault if you encourage him. I won't be held to blame. Well I'm off.'

'We ought to have made an impression of that key in soap,' said Richard, when they had heard the front door bang. 'And what on earth was all the rest of it about? D'you think she's a bit mad?'

But Laura had a very strange look in her eye. Instead of answering she said, 'Richard, I didn't have any nasty dreams last night, or the night before. Did you?'

Richard stared. Just for a moment it flashed into his mind that no, he had not had such a bad night as usual.

'And I told you, when I was sitting on the wall. I wasn't frightened on my own this morning. Don't you get it?'

Richard didn't 'get it' at all. It sounded to him like the beginning of another fairy story, like the goblin that broke the dinner plate. Laura stared at his blank, disapproving face. Then she gave one of her misunderstood groans.

'Oh, I give up. But if you want to know how the jug got broken, look outside on the step.' She stalked out of the room.

'Kids!' muttered Richard. But when Mrs Garth said 'him' she had jerked her head at the back door. Richard went to it and looked out. There was nothing to explain the hints. Only the saucer that Mum always left now for the stray cat. He noticed that it was empty.

Laura didn't go to school in town. She was in her last year at primary school, and went to the local school. Usually, the bus carried her from the bottom of the hill and back, but one day soon after this chat with Mrs Garth she came walking home to Cauld in the middle of the day. Mr Midfirth came out of his office as she passed:

'You're home early today?'

'It's a crisis,' said Laura. 'They've never had to switch the heating on so early, but they had to, and something was wrong with it and there was hot water everywhere. So they had to send us home anyway. We might be off for days.'

Mr Midfirth said, 'Aye. This weather'll cause everyone about a peck of trouble. Look at my scabious, and my young cabbage.' The stationmaster had a well-tended garden on the far side of the track, which was looking very brown and shrivelled and sad.

'Maybe it's just another Cauld clash,' suggested Laura, 'and it'll go away again.'

'Maybe,' said Mr Midfirth, 'but a Cauld clash is one thing. Ice in my fire buckets in October is something else again.'

He gave her a long serious look then, and said, 'So you'll be alone up there, eh?' He thought about this for a minute and then said, 'Stop there,' and disappeared into his office.

Laura wondered what he was fetching. Maybe it was a cosh, to use against burglars. But it wasn't. It was a book in a brown paper wrapper.

'You'll want something to occupy your mind,' he said. 'Take care.'

Laura went upstairs and sat on her bed. She didn't like what Mr Midfirth had said – 'You'll need something to occupy your mind.' It gave her the idea that her mind was in danger of being occupied by someone or something else, if she didn't keep it full up herself. And that was too close to the bad dreams for comfort. But it is better now, she reminded herself. It really was better, her bedroom felt quite friendly. She sat still and listened to the quiet house. Why weren't the builders working? Why had she seen no people about in Number Three's garden? Laura decided not to bother about it, and lay down with Mr Midfirth's book. She dozed, wondered about the builders, and fell asleep in earnest.

When the others came home they found three broken cups, and the dining-room furniture pushed about as if someone had been trying to rearrange it. Laura said that she hadn't heard a thing.

Strangely enough, not even Mum and Dad seemed to think Laura could be playing tricks this time. Richard heard them discussing the breakages.

'It's malicious,' said Mum.

'I can hardly credit it,' said Dad. 'But I'm beginning to think you must be right.'

They shut up when they saw Richard.

Next morning, everybody but Laura had gone to school or work. She sat at her bedroom window, reading. The stationmaster's book was not about growing cabbages, as she had feared. It was called *Curiosities of Cauld House Moor*. Quite a lot of the stories weren't really local, they were just folk tales and legends from all about the north of England. But in a chapter on unsolved mysteries, there was a story about a Victorian pot-holer who vanished one day, and his dog sat and howled outside Cauld House Farm for weeks. Under the heading 'Vanished Landmarks' there was a mention of the plaque that used to be on the road near Cauld, with a list of the people who had disappeared carved on it. But the village people made the Careys remove it. In a section on the Lancashire witches, she found the name Carey again. The Mr Carey of long ago, who built the house, was supposed to have done black magic in his cellar. ('That's why Mrs Garth was scared,' thought Laura.) They said that when he died he 'didn't need burying'.

Laura went through the book carefully, picking out these snippets. One of them made her grin and nod. It confirmed her suspicions about the 'stray cat' and the breakages. The strange thing was that the only entry boldly under the title 'The Secret of Cauld House' was about the underground river Dad had mentioned. Apparently you had only to follow the river and you would find the legendary treasure.

'That's very odd,' muttered Laura, 'very odd indeed.'

At the back of the book there was a slip of paper stuck in between two pages. It said: 'This copy not for sale. Limited Edition with private material. Author's family only. Three(3).'

'I wonder is Mr Midfirth descended from the Careys,' thought Laura.

After the slip came something that must be the private material. It was another story, but it didn't seem to belong with the rest. Laura flipped through it eagerly, but then she stopped and went back, with a puzzled frown, to the start of the different pages. But just then she heard the front door opening. Mrs Garth. Laura marked her place and quietly crept downstairs.

When Richard came in, she was reading the book again. 'Listen,' she said, and began to read him bits of the story at the back. There was a prince, and a treasure and a promise. There was the eerie Winter's Daughter, leaving a shining blight of ice on everything she touched. There was a beautiful picture of a tall wooden hall, with snow all round it and some purple hills beyond. The people in the picture had long braided fair hair, and rich-coloured clothes and jewels.

'It's a myth and legend isn't it?' said Laura. 'I don't see how it fits in with the rest,' she went on thoughtfully. 'D'you think it might somehow be the same treasure, brought here by the Vikings? Maybe it's in code.'

'Code?'

'Yes. You know, every tenth word and it tells you where the treasure is, or something.'

'That's an idea, Laur,' said Richard. 'What a nice storybook it is. When the weather's better we can have some fun looking for that treasure, can't we?'

'Fun!' said Laura.

Richard wondered what had got into her. She looked as if he'd said something really stupid, but he was only trying to cheer her up by joining in her make-believe. He left her with her book. Laura sat staring after him. She looked worried and unhappy.

That evening, it all came out. It began quietly. Mum and Dad were muttering about the broken pots and walking chairs. They were saying to each other that it would be very unpleasant trying to sort it out. As they talked, they glanced every now and then at the wall between Number One and Number Three. There were no bangs this evening; eveything was very quiet. Richard overheard bits of the discussion. He heard Mum say, 'Really, Dick, this place just hasn't suited us. Is it worth fighting?'

It was then that Laura started telling them about the boggart. She broke in on Mum and Dad, saying they'd 'got it all wrong', rushed off and came back with her book. She started reading out a passage about 'The Boggart of Cauld House':

'It breaks things, but it's *friendly*. The Careys always got on with it. Why can't we? Don't you see? It's *since*

the things started being broken that the bad feelings
have gone away. You *must* have noticed.'

Mum looked at Richard, who shrugged his shoulders
– it was nothing to do with him. Dad said, 'That's an
interesting-looking book, Laur. Can I have a closer look
at it?'

Laura looked from one face to another, saw their
indulgent, disbelieving expressions and suddenly, to
everyone's astonishment, she burst into tears.

'Laura! What's the matter?'

'It's her. It's her,' sobbed Laura. 'She's making you
not believe me. She gets at us through the walls. She's
occupying your minds, I know she is. She's making our
house horrible. She's made Richard so he doesn't even
care about the treasure and the Vikings.'

It was true that everyone had been unhappy about
the house, and their neighbours, for a long time, but it
was horrible to find that poor Laura had been getting
into such a state. Dad put her to bed. Richard was left
with Mum, in the kitchen, and now Mum said openly
that she and Dad thought Laura was – in a way – quite
right.

'We're quite convinced it's those Shores who are
playing tricks. It's too much of a coincidence that we
start having these "accidents" just when they start
rebuilding. But all this business about witchcraft and
nightmares is very worrying. It makes me think. Dad
and I have been thinking already, Richard, that perhaps
this move was simply a bad idea. This place is so lonely,
and – what do you think about it?'

Just then a stone tumbled, outside. Mum got up and
quietly opened the back door. Light streamed down the
garden and caught – Edith Shore, bending over the
Pledges' wall. She was wearing gardening gloves, and

carrying a length of clothes-line. When she saw she was caught she didn't say anything, didn't try to explain. She just stared, then turned and disappeared into the dark.

'I've spotted her creeping about like that before,' said Mum. 'No wonder Laura's frightened. Well, Dad and I must make up our minds whether Cauld House is worth the Shores. Meanwhile, you keep an eye on Laura. Don't let her do anything silly.'

Laura woke up in the dark. Her room seemed very cold. She got up and felt the storage heater – dead. Richard must have forgotten to turn them on again. She padded along to the bathroom, to get a blanket from the airing-cupboard. She didn't switch on the light, and so she could see that something was happening in the Shores' back garden. There was a torch bobbing about. Laura crept up to the window and peered out. There were two people – no, there were three people. One of them was very small. The Shores had got it between them. It was struggling and biting. Laura watched, fascinated and frightened: the thing kept fighting, and Laura found herself hoping desperately that it would get away. 'Come on,' she muttered, 'bite them.' But then the door of Number Three opened. Someone was standing there. When the captive saw the girl in the doorway it stopped fighting. It hung its head, cringing, and let Tom and Edith do what they liked.

Richard came awake, startled, to find his sister shaking him. 'Richard, Richard!' she hissed excitedly. 'They've got our boggart! They're tying him up with the clothes-line.'

It was some fantastic story about Ally, and the Shores, and someone being mistreated. It took him ages to persuade her she was dreaming, and get her back to bed.

Dad came in to Laura on his way out to work. He was surprised to find her still in bed.

'I'm getting up in a minute,' she said, in a rather weary voice.

'Stay there if you like. You look as if you need a bit more sleep. Good job you've got this holiday. Laura, where's the book you showed us last night? I want to tell you something about it.'

He sat down on the edge of the bed and carefully took the brown wrapper off Mr Midfirth's book. The name of the author, on the front and on the spine, was Gertrude Carey.

'Carey!'

'Yes. I thought you'd be interested. The Careys of Cauld House. You see we used to have a copy of this at home, I mean my home, Laur. Yes, it was just like this. I remember the story about the ice princess. I used to love that story. Didn't bother much about the rest – the print's too small. My grandad really valued that book, but something happened before it got passed on to me. I think my dad sold it. Pity. I wonder if Mr Midfirth might part with this one. Well, I have to go. See you later.'

Laura lay and gazed at the ceiling. She thought of the family that lived on Cauld House Moor and guarded something for hundreds and hundreds of years. 'Maybe we're part of that family. Maybe we are the last distant cousins of the Careys.' All the people who 'disappeared' were following the clue that Gertrude Carey had put in her book, for anybody to read: 'Some say that the

53

underground river is the answer to the riddle, and anyone who follows it will find the treasure chamber.'

'I don't believe it,' said Laura to herself. 'Why is this house built like a fortress? Why is it here at all?'

Laura did not want to go treasure hunting by herself. But if nobody would believe her she would have to find out the secret alone. She was afraid to wait any longer. She got dressed and then took from between her mattress and the bedstead a large, blackened key. She had not been able to work out what to do *after* 'making an impression in soap' so she had simply stolen it.

A few minutes later she was in the cellar. It was as blank and empty and bare as before. Laura tapped and twisted and poked all round the walls, but the secret door did not reappear. She sat on the bottom of the steps, chin in hand, and wondered what else to try. She found herself staring at a particular flagstone. She and Richard had prised at one or two of them – but surely their fingernails couldn't have left scratches on the stone?

Someone had been in the cellar since. Someone had been working with a knife blade, to get one of the flagstones up. Laura felt cold with a sudden fear that she was too late already. She knew she couldn't do anything without a tool, so she jumped up and ran to fetch one.

Laura was not the only person who had been waiting for Mrs Garth's day off. She had scarcely left the cellar before something happened to the partition wall. A section of it shifted, and was moved from behind.

Laura was buried in the cupboard under the stairs, searching frantically for a chisel. She got one out, and kneeled in the dark cupboard, biting her lip. She couldn't bear to think she might prise up that slab and find a secret hidden stone safe underneath – already empty. Then she heard footsteps, right over her head.

It couldn't be Mrs Garth; she never came on Thursdays. Anyway, Laura would have heard anyone coming in the front door. She stood up carefully, hefting her chisel.

Laura followed the footsteps upstairs. She crept along the landing in time to see her own bedroom door just closing. There was complete silence. She wondered if she had imagined the footsteps, and a draught had closed her door. After standing for a few moments listening to nothing, she went quietly along to the door and pushed it. She saw her empty room – her bed still rumpled. Everything seemed just as she'd left it. But the windows were wide open!

'Oh!' cried Laura, and jumped across to them.

She was just leaning out, peering at the garden and the cold hard earth below the window ledge, when – snick – the bedroom door closed quietly behind her. Laura gasped, spun round and ran out again. Too late. She pelted down the stairs, but the intruder was nowhere to be seen. She flung open the front door.

Mr Pledge worried about Laura all morning. He thought she'd looked feverish, as if she was sickening for something. He managed to get away from his school at lunchtime, to check on her. He stopped his bike in front of the house, took off his helmet and at once heard that someone was making a tremendous row round at Number Three. It wasn't the builders. He hurried to see, and found his daughter, armed with a chisel, hammering furiously at the Shores' door, yelling something about witches and burglars.

'Laura! What on earth are you doing?'

'She's been in my room! She's been doing something horrible.'

The door opened. Edith Shore stood there.

'What is the meaning of this?' She sounded indignant. However, she looked rather flustered.

'It's her!'

'Hush, Laura. I'm sorry, Edith. Laura's not too well today. I think she got lonely by herself.'

Edith seemed to have forgotten she was 'Auntie Edith'. She said, unpleasantly, 'If you can't control your children, Mr Pledge, *someone else may*. Take care this child doesn't interfere with me again.'

Laura burst into tears. Edith slammed the door.

'Come on, Laur,' said Dad. 'It's all right. I'm not cross with you.'

They believed her story. They didn't laugh the way they'd laughed at the boggart. By that evening Richard and Mum and Dad were full of ideas about how the 'haunting' had been done:

'Creeping about with a clothes-line – that was probably some trick for twitching things about and making weird shadows. As to the cellar, do you remember, Laur, I said there was something funny? It was too *clean*. Of course they'd been keeping it dusted so as not to leave footprints.'

It was decided that Mrs Garth would not be coming to Number One again. Perhaps she just 'didn't want to interfere'.

But she must have suspected something. And who else had that key?

To everyone's surprise Laura, the heroine of all the excitement, did not seem very interested. She put herself to bed early, of her own accord. When Richard came in to talk she just lay there looking miserable.

'Edith wasn't burgling to break things,' she said, in a tired voice.

'Well, whatever for then? We've counted the spoons.'

'Oh, I don't know. Bits of hair.'

'Bits of *hair*?' Richard couldn't understand. 'Listen, Laura – it was just bullying, to get us out of the way of their precious shop. Now they're found out it won't go on. There won't be any more broken jugs, I promise you.'

Laura said, 'It's much colder tonight.'

'Oh, d'you think so? I thought it was about the same.'

'I meant in here.'

5   Bewitched

'Daddy, did someone called Pledge marry someone called Carey years and years ago?'

Laura was ill. Her school was back to normal, but Laura stayed at home. She felt tired and low and helpless. Her parents kept her in bed, and said it was the flu. Her father had been telling her a story.

'You're thinking of that book,' he said. 'Well, where is it? Let's get it out and I'll read you some local legends.'

'Must be on my shelf,' said Laura.

Daddy started to look, saying, 'No. That's not how it was. There were two daughters in the end, Carey daughters. All the rest of the family had faded away. No cousins or aunts or uncles anywhere in sight. One of the daughters married. The two of them agreed they'd be called Carey, so the ancient name wouldn't die out. But her father and her elder sister wouldn't allow it. Like royalty you know. The couple were to give themselves a name that would remind them, not the precious noble name of Carey, but Pledge. They had to agree, because there was money in it, I think. The idea was, they were bound by this "Pledge" to come back and live here, if Gertrude died without children, which she did. It never happened. I think my great-gran and grandad were really offended about the name business, and never made it up. I haven't thought about it for years, that old story. I thought it was mainly just romancing. Did you know you have a school library book overdue here?'

'So the treasure belongs to us!'

Daddy grinned. 'Oh, so that's how your mind is working is it, young Laura? Well, I wouldn't count on it. "Treasure" hardly comes into my vague recollections of the story. Only something up here that the Careys were responsible for. A lot more trouble than it was worth. If there'd been anything you could dig up and put in the bank, I think my great-gran would have been keener to keep her "Pledge", don't you? I'm afraid I can't seem to see it.'

'Try under the bed.'

But Gertrude Carey's book had disappeared.

Richard stepped out of the front door and shuddered to the backbone as bitter frosty air swallowed him whole. Ally Shore was sitting on the wall in front of Number Three, in her school blouse and gym-slip, waiting for Edith to bring the car round. Richard generally managed to avoid meetings like this, and Ally never seemed interested in such encounters either, but this morning she said: 'Good morning, Richard Pledge.'

'Hallo,' said Richard reluctantly.

'Where is Laura Pledge?'

'She's not well. She's staying at home.'

'Ah! Ill in bed. A bottle for cold feet. Is that right? She doesn't like my weather, I think?'

'*Your* weather?'

There was a hard frost; it had been building up for a few days, more like February than October.

'My favourite weather. It comes as I want it.'

Richard said (he hardly knew why), 'Is that what the sparrow was for?'

Ally's colourless eyes opened wide, and then she laughed: 'Ah! I was behaving like a child then. I could not help myself, you know. I am better now. Well, here is Aunt Edith. Would you like a lift, Richard Pledge?'

Richard said, 'No.' He was very surprised to be asked. He wondered if Ally didn't know about the burglary business. He stood and watched the car go by before he started down the cold hill himself. He thought, seeing the two heads through the back window, that Edith must be sitting very low in her seat. Unless Ally had grown.

After school that afternoon Richard Pledge turned up at chess club for the first time in weeks. He had hardly started to play when Dr Radleigh swooped down and sent his opponent away. She said she wanted to find out if Master Pledge really was too good for the club these days. 'Sorry, mate,' muttered the opponent as she was swept aside.

'Well, Richard. How are you settling in on Cauld House Moor?'

It was clear that she knew he had come to chess club for a purpose, not just to play. Richard didn't know how to begin. But on this problem she seemed the best person to ask for advice.

'Oh well, all right, I suppose. It's not the moor I'm worried about . . .'

'Worried?' said Dr Radleigh gently. Richard seemed to have forgotten what he was going to say. He made a determined effort, and came out with:

'Well. It's Laura, my sister. She's behaving very strangely. In the first place it's a lot of talk about witches and haunting and treasure and goblins. Well, that's all right, she's always been imaginative. But now she's getting so scared of these ideas that she's making herself ill. She keeps bursting into tears and accusing us of – well, of course we don't believe her. It's so unlike

Laur. And then . . . you know we live next door to that strange girl called Ally Shore? Well, she never talks to me, but this morning she asked me where Laura was. Now why should she do that? I think she's been getting at Laura in some way. Have you seen the way the other first years do whatever she tells them? Laura came to me in the middle of the night, for instance, with some fantastic story about . . . I think it was Ally being done over by her auntie, and tied up. Obviously she tells Laur these stories about her aunt being a witch, to make herself important.'

He stopped, realizing that he had been getting carried away. Dr Radleigh looked thoughtful, and picked up a pawn.

'What about your grown-up neighbours?' she inquired, unexpectedly. 'How do you get on with them?'

Richard laughed and shook his head. 'Not very well. We've just had a big row with them actually. But it's nothing serious.'

He explained the story of the tricks the Shores had played. 'Obviously they want the whole farmhouse for their shop. And then, when Mum and Dad went round to have it out with them, they started attacking Mum about a stray cat, which they say is theirs, and she shouldn't feed it. They've really got a nerve. But the point is Laura won't listen to sensible explanations. She says Edith's a witch, and she's "doing horrible things to us", and it's all because of the Viking treasure.'

'Richard,' interrupted Dr Radleigh gently, 'what are your parents going to do about the criminal harassment you have suffered from the Shores?'

Richard stared at the chess board. He felt suddenly very confused. After a few moments he said, slowly: 'There's no point in taking it seriously. It would be such a lot of effort, and the truth is we don't even like the place much. The truth is, we probably won't do anything much. There's no point. Dad was going to talk to the agents about getting out of the lease anyway. We may as well just ignore the other business.'

'Breaking and entering? Criminal damage? Threatening behaviour? Richard, what do you think? Are your parents usually the sort of people who would calmly forget about that sort of persecution?'

The chess pieces seemed to dance under Richard's eyes. He was thinking of shadows and whispers. The bad dreams that he could never remember except that he woke up feeling he *must* get away from Cauld House. How do you organize that sort of harassment? Not with a clothes-line.

'Oh,' he said, with a nervous laugh. 'But that's silly. If we really were being bewitched, Laura wouldn't be the one worst off. She's suspected them all along.'

'No,' said Dr Radleigh. 'That is a false assumption. You surely must have heard of witch-doctors who can will a person's death *so long as the subject knows the intention and believes in the power*. Have you watched a judo class, Richard? There is little you can do with ju-jitsu if your enemy just walks by. It is when they see your threat, and attack, or try to, that you can throw them to the ground. Do you see what I mean?'

She was speaking very quietly. When she stopped, the busy silence of the chess club seemed noisy. Richard was hanging his head, as if he'd just been lectured for making some stupid moves. At last he said:

'This morning I went to see Laur before I came out. She told me about a dream. She dreamed she could see through the wall behind her bed, and Edith Shore was there, sitting in the dark. She was winding something in her hands. Not winding a clock; thread on a spindle, like when you fly a kite. Laur said she thought Edith's thread was being pulled out of her.'

Dr Radleigh said, 'I have heard of similar dreams. Yes.'

'But, Dr Radleigh, what *about* Ally? Where does she fit in?'

Dr Radleigh picked up her pawn again. She and Richard had been moving almost at random, and their board was looking disorganized. She put the piece down, a step further on its way.

'I don't know,' she said, 'just what to think about Ally. She is certainly a stranger, but she took our salt, didn't she? She looks out of mirrors as well as into them, she has no sinister prejudices against iron or running water. And think, Richard. What she said to you this morning could have been a warning just as well as a taunt. It is very possible that she can't help her company, and would change it if she could. Let us leave her in peace – I hate to condemn someone just for being unusual. This other pair, however, must be stopped. Let me see. It is against my general rule, but I think in this case I could give you a simple charm. If it works, the business is over. If not – well, we'll think about that when we need to. Come down to my office when you've helped to put these tables away. If I'm not there, I'll be in the garden, or the small sewing-room.'

Around them, the chess club was beginning to clear itself away, with a normal cheerful bustle of rattling pieces and scraped chairs and chatter.

The doctor came to see Laura on Saturday morning. It was unheard of for Laura to be ill more than a week, and her family were really worried. Richard watched

Dad and the doctor coming out of Laura's room. The doctor was murmuring about Laura settling in at her new school — was she having problems?

'Just keep her warm and quiet. Brr — if you can. It really is freezing up here, isn't it? I've heard about Cauld House Moor, but I didn't believe it till today.'

Richard let them get downstairs, and went in to Laura. She was just lying there, gazing listlessly at the ceiling. Richard fingered something in his jeans pocket, and frowned. He had been trying to make up his mind about this 'something' since he came home from school last night. He went over to the window. The doctor was right, it was very cold today. The sky was thick and livid and yellow like a bruise.

'Have you seen the weather?' he said. 'Mr Midfirth said yesterday that it would snow. I think he might be right.'

Even as he spoke, the first few heavy and aimless-looking white fragments drifted past the window.

'Laura! It *is* snowing. Aren't you interested?'

The flakes tumbled gently; not very many of them. Richard began to sing, to encourage them, the old north country rhyme Dad had taught them long ago:

'Ally, Ally, Aster,
Snow, snow faster.
If you don't
I'll tell thy master.'

But Laura didn't respond. She just sighed and said, 'I wish you wouldn't sing that.'

Richard came and sat on the edge of the bed. He said, 'Laura. Will you tell me truthfully? Have you been talking to Ally Shore? Is she the one who told you her aunt is a witch, and frightened you?'

'I never talk to Ally,' she said dully. 'Haven't you noticed? Ally just disappears when she comes home. The witch only lets it out sometimes, for a treat I suppose.'

'*It?*'

Laura was feeling too ill and tired to hide even her worst ideas from anyone just now. 'Yes. Witches always have one. I suppose they know the kids at your school are too big and stupid to guess. I touched her once. She was getting out of the car as I walked by. She's not warm. She's cold. She's not human. She's the thing the witch uses. They always have one.'

Richard had heard enough. Anything that would save Laura from these horrible ideas was worth trying. He took out of his pocket the 'simple charm' that Dr Radleigh had given him. It was a necklace, of berries threaded on a strand of red silk.

'Laura, you're not to show this to anyone. It's, it's a sort of herbal medicine. Someone at school said it might do you good.'

Laura sat up. 'It's a rowan ring!' she cried. 'It's rowan berries, to protect against witches. I've read about them. Oh, Richard! You believe me!'

'I don't . . .' began Richard, but he couldn't wipe that smile of relief and delight off her face, '. . . know what to believe,' he finished lamely. 'Try wearing it, anyway.'

The snowflakes were falling slower now, but Richard didn't sing the rhyme again.

That night Laura had a new dream. She was standing in the bathroom again, and she was looking out of the window. She could see a patch of light on the dark wall of Number Three. A little window: there was a face at the window. She could see a wide open mouth: Help! Help! She seemed to be very close to the prisoner. She could see its pointed teeth and its huge round eyes. Then the little face jerked and two large dark hands appeared, shutting its mouth. 'Gardening gloves,' said Laura, and woke to find herself standing in darkness, with cold tiles under her feet, and the rowan ring clutched tightly in her hands.

'They've got someone locked up in there! I know they have!'

Laura was certainly a lot better now she had the 'charm'. The trouble was, she was convinced that Richard believed all her horror stories now, and every moment that she caught him alone she started talking about the witch next door, and rescuing the 'boggart', and saving the Carey treasure. Richard didn't dare to tell her he really thought it was all psychological, and she was getting better because she *thought* the charm worked. He tried hinting something, and Laura immediately said, 'All right. I'll take it off,' and fetched the wizened string out of her pyjamas, where it was hidden around her neck. She looked angry and defiant. She'd probably get ill again just to spite him.

'No, don't do that.'

'You're just a coward. You do believe it is witches, and a boggart, but you just don't want anything to happen.'

In the end, to keep her under control, he had to make a bargain. If she promised not to try and get into the Shores' house herself, then next Saturday, when Mum and Dad weren't around, he would do the burgling himself.

'And probably find your "prisoner" is Mum's stray cat "locked up" in a basket.'

'No you won't.'

'We'll see. There's only one condition, Laura. You've got to find a way to make sure the Shores are out on Saturday morning. Otherwise the plan's off.'

The doctor found Laura much better on Monday, but said she'd better stay off school for a few more days, especially since the weather was so bad. Saturday's snow was just a sprinkle, but on Tuesday there was a real fall, even in town. Richard came home reporting snowball fights outside Morrison School, and great excitement. But it couldn't last. On Wednesday the snow was soft; by Thursday it was gone, and the moor was brown again. Laura, who was watching the weather carefully, noticed that it was very much colder around the house on the moor at night than in the daytime, but she didn't think this was important at the time. She was just hoping for fine weather, frosty or warm.

On Thursday Laura took a quiet convalescent stroll out over the moor. She didn't think she was breaking the law, because she wasn't alone. Tom and Edith Shore were always in view. They were strolling too. It crossed Laura's mind that this would be a perfect opportunity to sneak into Number Three. But she had promised Richard, and, besides, she was interested in the strange way the Shores were behaving. They kept stopping and peering at the ground. Laura sneaked closer. She crept from boulder to boulder and finally was caught by surprise at the sound of voices right in front of her. Peering through a crack between two stones she could see two pairs of feet. Edith had a walking stick, the kind that ends in a metal point. She was poking it into the ground.

'It's for the best, in any case. We should have realized,

making the girl ill is a nuisance, not an advantage. We don't want her around the house.'

Laura clutched at her rowan ring, and held her breath. 'I wish Richard could have heard that,' she thought.

The footsteps moved off slowly. When they were well away Laura came out of hiding. She had to look for quite a while before she could work out what Edith had been poking at. There was a crack in the rock. There were lots of cracks and hollows and holes, but Laura realized eventually that this one was deeper and darker than the others. Something glinted, far inside. Laura dropped a pebble and heard a tiny 'chink' after a second or so, as if it had struck glass. 'Brrr.' The air that came up from out of that mysterious split was very cold indeed.

She stayed where she was, and watched Tom and Edith slowly wandering back to the road. They kept stopping and poking occasionally all the way. When they were safely out of sight she tried to trace their path. It was soon clear – they were following the cracks in the ground, the special cracks that were very cold and dark. There was even one of these in the old tarred surface of the road. It wasn't just a sign of age and neglect; it was new and sharp, as if something inside had swollen up and was splitting the ground like a chick splitting an eggshell.

Laura went into the house, making sure she wasn't seen as she passed Number Three. She sat thinking for a while. Then she jumped up. She wanted to check her theory by having another look at the book of Cauld House Curiosities. Then she remembered that that book had not been seen since the day Edith Shore came visiting without an invitation. She sat down again, smiling rather grimly. Now she knew a certain way to lure the Shores out of their house. But what about Ally?

'Oh, you needn't worry about Ally,' said Richard. 'She's out of the way already.'

'What d'you mean?'

'I'm sorry. I should have told you. It was when we had the snow. It was much thicker around our school, you know, than anywhere else in town. Everyone was outside at four o'clock, fooling about in it. Ally was there too. I saw her standing out on the pavement without her coat. She's always doing things like that, she's teaching all the first years to be Spartans, I think. Edith and Tom arrived and got out of the car and started lecturing her and asking her how she expected to get away with acting like that. Ally said 'Oh, I can't help it' or something, and they were really annoyed. I couldn't stay close without them noticing, but there was more. I thought I heard them say they were sending her away until the weather was better. Then today she didn't turn up. I remembered our burglary, so when she wasn't at assembly I asked her teacher. It was all right – he only thought it was about a lift home. Apparently she's gone to visit some relations. She goes to see them every month, or she's going to in future. I wonder why it's allowed. Anyway, I must have heard them saying she mustn't catch cold and spoil her visit. So that's that. The coast's clear.'

Laura said, 'It's allowed because Edith makes people think whatever she wants. But I wish we'd seen her go.'

On Friday evening the Pledge children were taking a short walk round their garden. They paced up and down, talking secrets, ignoring the sharp cold of the evening. Richard had an eye on the construction of scaffolding and tarpaulin that shrouded the front of the house next door. Soon he saw what he was waiting for – a furtive movement.

'OK,' he breathed, and then went on, in a rather careless whisper, 'it sounds dangerous, Laura. We ought to tell Mum and Dad.'

'But they'd never let us do it,' protested Laura, too excited to lower her voice. 'They don't even believe in the treasure.'

'How can you be so sure you'll find your way through, underground?'

'How can I get lost if I'm following a river? We'll do it just as we planned. I'll trail a clue behind me, *and* I'll make sure you can follow me above ground as well. I'll be like Theseus in the maze. Besides, you'll know where I am heading.'

Her voice dropped again, and the Pledge children went back into their house.

Outside in the garden, the air was frosty after a mild day. Inside Number Three, the cold was far worse. But Tom and Edith were afraid of upsetting their young friend if they didn't give her some freedom. So, for an hour or two in the evenings, they endured the third and worst 'Cauld clash' so far, behind thickly drawn curtains and tightly closed doors. Tom was worried about Laura.

'Isn't it a bit funny that she's stumbled on it, when we've been looking and looking and never found a way down?'

'She's a bit too knowing,' agreed Edith. 'But that's all the more reason to take advantage of this short cut. My idea is, we watch her until she shows us the place. We suddenly appear, and if she doesn't run off straight away, for fear of giving away the secret, we can soon make a little girl see reason. Can't we?'

She winked, and made a sort of gesture with her hands, like someone winding up a bobbin.

'Oh, I get you,' said Tom. 'More of the same.'

'I may have to bring her back to the house, while you make sure of the hoard. Or – well, it doesn't matter. It will be simple enough. The other seekers most probably drowned, you know. But we've no fear of that.'

'Brr, no.'

Ally sat by the fire, which could not warm anyone, but which made the Shores feel better. She listened to the plotting, and smiled. She did not think the river would lead them anywhere. But it didn't matter. Soon there would be no more secrets, and nothing would be buried deep enough to be hidden. It was only a case of waiting for the right season. Tom and Edith did not understand. Eventually they would have to realize the truth, but for the moment Ally was very happy to leave them to their plots and schemes and conjuring tricks. Her time would come. The fire, a hearty heap of wood and coal, suddenly gave a sort of moan. Its last lingering flames turned blue and disappeared. The room became violently cold.

'I think,' said Ally diffidently, 'the moon must have risen.'

'Right, madam,' said Edith with a chuckle. 'Time you were tucked up in your little bed, eh?'

'I think,' said Ally, standing up, 'I think you'd better put me right away, Auntie Edith. Until after the turn, this time.'

She went to the door like an obedient child, icy air flowing from her as she moved. Edith gave Tom a wink and a nod behind the creature's back: everything was under control.

'You go and check up on our other pet,' she said. 'Tell him we've found our own way in. That'll frighten him, the obstinate little beast.'

6 *Unbewitched*

Even after the eavesdropper in the garden, Richard wasn't entirely convinced that the Shores would trail after Laura. Nor was he very happy about seeing Laura go off on to the moor alone. But he was certain that she must not be the one to invade Number Three, and he was also certain that if he didn't keep his promise now she would make her own arrangements. He watched her leave from his bedroom window. She had promised not to go further than a particular ridge they both knew, the last before the great swell of the real hills. And she'd promised to stay on paths they had both followed. Laura's back went down the road in a red anorak. It disappeared round a bend. Immediately, up popped two Shores. One minute they were invisible, the next minute they were in the road. Richard laughed: they must have crawled from their garden on their hands and knees! Well well, so they really are treasure seekers. How funny! He was relieved. Laura certainly wasn't going to be alone out there.

Laura was perfectly all right. The plan was that she must keep the Shores away from the house until noon. At twelve o'clock Richard would give up his burgling and get clear, whether he had found the 'prisoner' or not. No matter where the Shores were, Dad would be back from his fortnightly staff meeting by lunchtime, and *he* mustn't know anything about this. 'The difficult bit,' thought Laura, 'is going to be keeping them on the move. They've been prowling around out here so much already they might get blisters and give up.' But she needn't have worried. The Shores were very persistent. Laura led them up and down the first stretch of moorland by the road, crossing and re-crossing Richard's 'arena'. She was pretending to be checking something marked or noted in the boulder-strewn ground. She was trying to follow, in fact, the Shores' own treasure trail.

'She's lost!' complained Tom. 'What's she up to? We've been all over here. There's nothing.'

Edith sat down and rubbed her gloved hand over the surface of the rock where they had halted.

'No,' she said. 'Not lost. Look at this. See; chalk. She's marking the river.'

'Why are you rubbing it out? It might come in useful for us too.'

Edith said, 'Don't you remember? This is her arrangement so the boy can follow her. So that she can't be lost.'

The brother and sister looked at each other thoughtfully. They had not discussed what they were going to do with the little girl if she didn't run off straight away, if she realized she had been trailed deliberately and that the secret of the treasure was discovered. Some things are best left to the inspiration of the moment.

It was half past ten. Laura decided it was time for a rest. She scrambled down into a little dent in the ground, a deep dimple as if someone had pushed a giant thumb into the moor. Up above her, she knew, there was a stand of dead and crackling bracken that was inhabited by two big and uncomfortable hounds. The hare was having fun. It was a beautiful bright clear autumn day, and she thought she would just sit here and enjoy it for a while. The heather was dry and springy to rest on. She slipped her little pack off her shoulders, and calmly took out a flask and a bar of chocolate. As she did so, she glanced up at the red bracken.

Edith grabbed Tom's arm and pulled him back. 'She saw you!'

There was no doubt of it. They wondered what the little girl would do. Tom peered through the stiff stems again, and saw Laura quietly sitting as before, sipping her hot drink. Silently, he moved back so Edith could see too. They realized immediately what this meant.

'She knew all along. She's been leading us a dance!'

They were furious. In angry whispers they discussed what to do. 'I'm going to go down there and give the young lady a good talking to,' said Tom. 'Cheeky little monkey! It's none of her business. It's *our* treasure!'

But Edith said. 'No. We can teach her a lesson without giving ourselves away. Or, supposing she really knows something, she will show us the way even though she never meant to.'

'Ah,' said Tom. 'I get you.'

'Just give me time to get back to the house. Then watch her, and make up your own mind, from the symptoms. If she runs, then you must follow her, and we've nothing more to lose, because she *knows*. If she wanders, she knows nothing. Let her go.'

'Just let her go, eh?'

'She shouldn't be out here alone. We can't help it if she misses her way, can we?'

'Or else follow her. And then?'

Edith didn't answer. It is sometimes best not to have everything cut and dried.

Laura was still having fun. She'd finished her chocolate, and started out again. This time she was making straight for the Pennines. She was still marking rocks, but not so carefully. It was past eleven, and she was sure that Tom and Edith were well hooked. All she had to do now was lose them, somewhere a good way away from the house. She went on for about half an hour. The steeply rising ground was so open she didn't dare look back much, but occasionally she had a chance to glimpse someone ducking out of sight, so that was all right. At last she reached the top of the last ridge. The great brown whaleback of moorland was topped with a huge, smooth boulder. If you climbed it you could see for miles and miles. Laura dropped down behind it now. She decided to have five minutes' rest and then start for home.

The dell where Laura had first rested wasn't very far, in a straight line, from Cauld House. Edith reached home.

Laura jumped up, and then pitched herself down again, amazed at herself. For Tom was right on top of the ridge behind, and looking straight in her direction. But she had suddenly had the most vivid impression that she *must* get back to the house. Was Richard in trouble? 'Stupid,' she muttered, but her hand felt for her rowan ring inside her scarf. Then she remembered that it wasn't there. The thread had snapped, and the berries were shrivelled and black anyway, so she'd left it off. But it didn't matter, she realized. Her job was done, and there was no need to stay out here. The important thing was to get back to the house.

At first, it was quite sensible. She tumbled and wriggled down the slope she'd climbed and when she was at the bottom she crept, ducking and weaving through the heather and the rocks, until she thought she'd passed Tom. She risked a peep, and there he was, standing by the boulder, apparently quite unaware that he was clearly outlined against the sky. Had he seen through the trick?

'It doesn't matter,' thought Laura. 'All that matters now is getting back to the house.'

She began to run. It was stupid to run; the ground was full of holes and littered with loose stones, and you could twist an ankle in the heather roots. She tried to stop herself – no need to get hot and bothered – but every time she started off again her knees felt weak and trembly, her legs insisted on breaking into a hurried, frightened trot. And, every time she looked behind, there was Tom. He never seemed to get any nearer or farther. He was always standing up against the sky, and the face she couldn't see was always staring straight at her. Laura's throat hurt, and in spite of the running, she began to feel cold.

'*Where's Edith!*' It was bad enough before, but after that thought came to her, it was a hundred times worse. Tom was behind her; she *must* get back to the house, and Edith was somewhere unseen, secretly hiding. Edith seemed about to jump out from behind every stone.

She had lost, without even realizing it, the path that she'd promised to follow, but at last, with a gasp of relief, she recognized ahead of her one of the stones she'd marked with her chalk. The sight of it put strength into her; her legs seemed her own again as she ran to it. 'I'm safe! I just have to follow the marks. Soon I'll be at the road.'

But she could not find her chalk cross. It was gone. And now she realized why she had been feeling so cold. The sun had disappeared. A white mist was gathering, and Tom was somewhere in it, close behind her. With a gasp, nearly a sob, Laura jumped to her feet and ran like the wind. She forgot everything now, why she was running or where. She only knew that she was pursued, and she had to get away. It was no use. She was young and quick, but it was as if she had weights tied to her heels. Soon she could hear him, crashing through the dry grass and pounding on the stones. The chase couldn't go on much longer. When the hunter was so close that she could hear his breath, Laura gave up. She fell down. She had stumbled often, but this time she had not the will to get her balance again, and she fell headlong, her face buried in dusty bracken. She could not run any more. She rolled over and got to her knees. Tom's face peered down at her, scarcely a foot away. She could see the grey and brown bristles on his chin; she could see the yellowish teeth in his grinning mouth.

'Heh, heh,' said Tom. 'Gotcha!' There was a twinkle in his eye. Two large hands reached out. Laura suddenly found she could move again.

'No!' she yelled, and flung herself sideways. For a moment he seemed to hang poised. She saw his astonished face, and then he was falling, tumbling, rolling head over heels down the steep hidden slope of the very dell where Laura had stopped to eat her chocolate.

When Laura managed to stop running again, she knew she was safe. He was gone. She sat down on the grass – it was very damp now – and stared about her. 'Goodness, it's quiet. I must have been crazy. I deserved to break a leg.' It was only then that she realized how thick and close the mist had fallen. She could not see anything she recognized. The stones she had marked were not marked any more.

'Oh help!' cried Laura, out loud. 'And on top of all that, now I'm lost!'

*

Richard sat on the edge of the bath, staring at the back wall of Number Three. It was half past ten, or thereabouts. Laura and the Shores must be well away, and he had better start his burglary soon. The two halves of the house each had a modern kitchen and bathroom built on to the old structure. He could just make out the little window Laura had told him of; it was high up in the angle between the new bit and the old, on the Shores' half. It seemed to be boarded up inside. It was so high and so small anyway that he didn't see how Laura could possibly have seen anything going on in there.

'Magic,' he murmured, and sighed.

He did not know what to believe about the Shores. The likeliest thing was still Mum and Dad's version; they wanted the whole of Cauld House for their shop, and they weren't too scrupulous about how they persuaded their unwelcome neighbours to leave. Dr Radleigh's suggestion was easily explained: It was a very good idea to make Laura think she had a 'cure' for witchcraft. And it was sensible of Dr Radleigh to point out to him how odd his parents' behaviour might look to someone too young to understand all the difficulties. Shadows and nightmares – Richard shook his head. No, it was too fantastic. He only hoped that Laura would be finally convinced, after this ridiculous burglary, and not get the two of them into any more trouble.

Scrambling over the low wall which divided the two properties was no problem. He had chosen the kitchen window for his break-in, because the catch was the same as the Pledges', and you could shift that, with luck, from the outside. But when he was closer he saw something much better. The top part of their bathroom window was ajar, and, temptingly close, there was a

79

sturdy drainpipe. Luckily he'd put on old jeans and a scruffy jumper. He took off his shoes and lost no time in shinning up the pipe. Soon he was descending head first into the Shores' bath, with a clatter of tumbling shaving creams, toothbrushes and general bathroom rubbish. He crouched in the tub, feeling horrified at the row, and for a moment he was sure the door would open and he'd be discovered, looking absolutely ridiculous. But no one came. He climbed out. He tried to clear up traces of rusty drainpipe and put the fallen things back. He noticed that there were only two toothbrushes. He wondered which of the Shores had dentures.

Number Three had fewer rooms than Number One. Upstairs there were just two bedrooms, besides the new bathroom. Downstairs, there was the modern kitchen, a fair-sized living-room looking very prim and unused, and a front room that must be in pieces at the moment, being converted into a shop. The whole house was extremely chilly, but naturally it would be while a wall was being knocked out.

Richard sat on a cold armchair in the Shores' parlour. He was surrounded by boxes. Some had been opened but none had been unpacked. Clocks, pinned butterflies, huge lumps of china. There was dust all over them, as well as over the stiff furniture. Richard wondered — mildly — why the Shores didn't take better care of their stock. He wondered whether he might go home. He had looked into every room but the one that was being taken apart, and it was all perfectly innocent. He knew where Laura's little window must be: it must be behind Edith Shore's wardrobe. He knew he really ought to go and shove that big heavy thing aside and make *sure* there was no secret locked door, but the idea of dragging furniture around in a strange lady's bedroom was too much for him to contemplate. Well, at least he could check out what the builders were really doing.

He went to the door of the front room. It was thickly padded with felt all round the edges, to keep the cold out of the rest of the house, presumably. But it isn't working, thought Richard. With his hand on the knob, it suddenly came to him that though the tarpaulin stayed up, and the van was always on the roadside, he hadn't heard any noise from over here for days and days. Of course, they knock off before we get home. But why leave the van? He opened the door and looked inside. His mouth dropped open.

No one had touched the front wall of Number Three. There was one little sash window, just as there had always been, gloomy now from the sheet of tarpaulin outside. There was no rubble. The wall was papered with a pattern of fat blue flowers. Richard stared at this untouched blank for several seconds, before he realized what was really happening in the Shores' front room. There were newspapers on the floor, and someone had taken up several floorboards. The top of a step ladder was poking out of the hole. There was a torch lying by the hole. Richard went over and picked it up, and shone it into the depths. Clearly Number Three didn't have any official access to the cellars of Cauld House, so the Shores had had to make their own way in. He could see the wooden partition, and the place where Tom and Edith had cunningly taken out a panel in such a way that they could put it back, without leaving a sign, in between their raids on Number One. He could also see what had caused the horrible hammering, banging and battering that had tormented the Pledges when the 'conversion' first began. The Shores had been breaking up the beautiful old slab pavement of their cellar floor. They had also dug quite a deep pit into the dirt underneath.

Piles of earth and digging tools lay abandoned. It looked as if the Shores had long given up that particular search. Richard switched off the torch and stepped away from the hole. He no longer thought it was very funny that Laura had led the Shores out treasure seeking. If the whole antique shop business was a fake, that meant the pair had gone to an immense amount of trouble already, for whatever they thought was buried on Cauld House Moor. An immense amount of trouble to keep a secret, and now they thought Laura knew . . .

When he looked again at the room, he saw that this was Tom and Edith's headquarters – rugs and jumpers, piles of fuel, and even a box of tinned food. 'Are they guarding their hole?' he wondered. But there was something more urgent to think about. He had to get out on the moor at once; he couldn't leave Laura to face two outraged Shores alone. He was making for the stairs, to leave by the bathroom again, when it suddenly occurred to him that he had missed something *very* odd on his first trip round the rooms. There was no place for Ally. There were only two bedrooms. He hadn't seen anywhere any arrangement for the girl, not even a camp-bed in a corner.

He gave up his rush to leave the house. He went and sat down in the parlour again, with his thoughts in a whirl. He had to believe in the treasure hunt now. What if the *whole* of Laura's version was true? He had a sudden image of himself talking to Dr Radleigh: *would your parents usually forget such persecution?* Edith and Tom Shore wanted the Pledges to move out, and the Pledges were ready to go. Not because of some broken crockery, not really. Because of the bad dreams, and the shadows, and a general, growing feeling that they would be better off elsewhere. Richard then had another, most unwelcome, thought. If Edith really was a witch, then maybe 'Alice Shore' really was a witch's familiar. She might still be in this house. She might just not be looking like a little girl today.

He jumped up. He had had enough thinking. He made for the stairs again, but not for the bathroom. He was going to tackle Edith's wardrobe.

He heaved and heaved, but the wardrobe would not stir. Inside it, something woke up. He heard it scrabble and whimper, and then a thin voice crying some indistinct – 'Never . . . won't . . . go away . . .' With that voice there was an end to all doubt. 'It's all right, boggart,' hissed Richard, jumping into the fairy tale, 'I'm not the witch. I'm a friend. Shut up, though. We may not be alone.'

But it didn't hear, or it didn't understand. It was making quite a row. 'Hush!' whispered Richard, expecting any second a white-faced thing that only looked like a girl to come up behind him and lay its cold, cold hand on him. He gave up shoving for a minute and opened the wardrobe door, so the prisoner could hear him better. Then he saw, between the folds of clothes, the bolts on the inside. He pushed away Edith's dresses and skirts (and some Morrison girl's school uniform). There was a door in the back of the wardrobe, where someone had sawn the real back away. It was heavily bolted, but there was a key in the lock. The Shores had not expected their prisoner to be helped from the outside. In a minute, though it must have seemed a lot longer to the creature crying and scrabbling inside, he had everything open, and the door gave way. Out pelted a small brown something.

Richard grabbed it. But it said, 'No, no! She's here!' and jumped away from him. Richard thought the thing meant Ally. But he didn't. He meant Edith. They'd both been making too much noise to hear her quietly come in downstairs, but to the wild creature her smell was strong enough. Richard hurried after the prisoner. When he came out of the bedroom he saw the boggart crouched half-way down the stairs, obviously watching something.

'Hey, boggart,' he hissed. 'Don't be stupid. We've got to get out of here!'

The boggart took no notice. Richard couldn't leave it to its fate. He crept down after it, and found himself looking into the parlour, from above; seeing what the boggart saw. It was not Ally. It was Edith. She was kneeling in front of a cabinet of polished wood, on legs. Richard had taken it for an old-fashioned TV. The doors were open now. There were dolls inside. The antique shop's collection of antique toys. Lying in the back was a really well made one: you could see the delicate porcelain face, and a floss of hair, though the rest of the figure was wrapped in paper. In front of the box there were four other dolls. These were very clumsy, crude-looking things, but someone had tried to dress them. Two had dark hair; just a few strands stuck on, like bits rescued from a comb. The other two were fair. Richard and his mother had dark hair. Dad and Laura were blond. One of the dark-haired dolls had a bit of paisley-patterned material wrapped around it. He could remember his mother saying 'Now where did I do that? I've torn my blouse.'

Three little helpless dummies sat in the front of the

84

cabinet. Edith had the fourth in her hands. She had a fine piece of wire, too, which she was warming over a candle flame, so when she wound it round the wax body it cut into the doll just a little. She was working carefully, reading from a book of instructions propped up against the legs of the cabinet. Her lips moved.

'Laura!' Richard was paralysed. He couldn't move or speak. He couldn't believe what he was seeing, he couldn't imagine what he could do to stop the witch. The boggart was not paralysed. It got up on top of the banister rail. Its teeth were chattering with fright, but suddenly, with a shriek, it launched itself into the air. It landed on Edith's shoulders, and sent her flying. In a flash, it grabbed up all four dolls in its mouth and its monkey hands. Edith was on her feet – but she was too late. The boggart had made another wild leap, and gone crashing through the window. Richard retired to the top of the stairs. When Edith's shouting had faded he quietly came down again, slipped out of the open back door, reclaimed his shoes, and was safe in Number One, watching through the kitchen window, when Edith reappeared a few minutes later, without her prisoner or her dolls. The wild moorland began right at the garden wall, and a white mist had suddenly sprung up. There was no chance of catching the boggart out there.

Laura got home only minutes before Dad. She found Richard at the gate.

'What are you all dressed up like that for?'

'To come looking for you, numbskull. Are you all right?'

'I am *now*.'

'Did you, ah – er – have any trouble?'

Laura looked at him suspiciously. There was something strange in his expression. 'There was a mist,' she

85

said cautiously. 'It came down in a minute. I thought I was lost. Then I heard something run past me, and I *thought* I heard a voice say, 'Sit tight.' So I did, and the mist went, and I was only in that place where the ditches are. Before that, it was horrible, because Tom chased me, and I couldn't get away from him, it was as if someone was pulling me back. But I don't suppose you care to hear about that.'

Richard swallowed. Possibly he was swallowing his pride. 'The mist,' he said steadily, 'was the boggart's business, I think. It helped it – him – to get away. It's no wonder, though, that you had trouble with Tom. Edith was back here, having another go at you. *Why* did you go out without the rowan ring, you idiot?'

Laura stared, and then slowly she began to smile.

'Go on,' said Richard. 'Call me whatever you like.'

But before she had time to start, they both heard the growl of Dad's bike coming up the hill. They hurried indoors. They had a lot to tell each other – in private.

Laura, up early on Monday morning and ready for school again, went out with a saucer of milk to the back doorstep, and found a message there. It was scratched with a burnt twig on the step. It said:

I ET THEM. BEST CURE

'Are you leaving out milk for the cat?' said Mummy's voice behind her.

Laura quickly scuffed over the marks with her shoe. 'Yes.'

'Good for you. The Shore woman has been over here

saying it's lost again. Apparently they had it shut up, and she seems to think one of you two let it out. Well, I hope you did. *And* I told her so. We've put up with quite enough nonsense from that pair.'

7 Threatening Weather

The tarpaulin disappeared from the front of Number Three, the builder's van Tom had hired was gone from the roadside. Tom himself was laid up. He had had a fall. Mr and Mrs Pledge were startled to see the intact wall, and asked themselves, 'Did we ever see those builders? Did we just assume they were there because of the noise?' Three Pledges cornered Edith getting out of her car after school one day. They found out that 'there was something wrong with the foundations, so the conversion can't be carried out as planned' (Richard and Laura sniggered rudely when they heard that). 'Oh dear,' said Dad coldly. 'What about your shop?' Edith was wearing dark glasses, which looked weird in the dusk. She glanced at the quiet, pale schoolgirl beside her and said: 'I think we'll be finished with this place by Christmas. Will you come inside, Ally?'

'She must be feeling low,' said Dad. 'She's even stopped bullying the little girl. What on earth was she doing in sunglasses? Looked as if she'd been in a fight.'

Mum and Dad both claimed they'd been on the point of writing to a lawyer, but it didn't matter now. Richard was rather disappointed that 'Ally Shore' didn't simply vanish after they'd beaten the witch. Instead she went on coming to school, behaving almost like any other first year. Perhaps she wasn't a familiar spirit, perhaps she was just an odd girl, being used as camouflage like the 'antique shop'. Dr Radleigh only mentioned the matter once. She met Richard in a corridor and said, 'Ah, Richard. Haven't seen you for a day or two. Did

you sort out that problem with your neighbours?'
Richard said, 'Yes' and she said, 'Good. Least said
soonest mended. We will forget about it.' With one
sharp look in his face she'd whisked away again.
Richard was glad. He didn't want to talk about wax
dolls and mutterings. One brush with magic had been
quite enough.

The Pledges couldn't find anyone to replace Mrs Garth,
which was rather annoying, but at least the weather
was better. This was very welcome, because the house
had turned out a draughty, chilly place. There didn't
seem any way to keep it warm. Richard and Laura got
into trouble for heaving up a flagstone in the cellar, and
their father proved to them conclusively that if the
Viking treasure was anything you could find like that it
would have been unearthed long ago. Laura said something about treasure seekers next door. 'More fool
them,' said Dad. 'If you ask me, I'm sure it's just a
parable.'

'A what? Oh, you mean like "Dig in the fields and
you'll get rich"?'

'That's the idea. Duty and loyalty, the value of family
traditions, kind hearts are more than coronets. Sorry,
Laura.'

The Pledges kept on leaving out milk for the 'cat',
who was known as Humphrey for some reason. The
milk vanished, but indoors there were no teacups
broken.

On November the fifth Laura and Richard went into
Cauld, and bought sparklers and some sausages and
potatoes. To their amazement two women who came
into the shop smiled at them, in an embarrassed way.

'Having a bonfire?' asked one.

'That's a good idea,' said the other. 'You have a good blaze up there, and a good lot of crackers.'

The Pledge children went away mystified: 'Why are they suddenly talking to us?'

'They sounded *sorry* for us. Cheek!'

'Maybe they feel guilty for being so unfriendly.'

They had a good bonfire anyway. Flames leaped and sparks sizzled. The Pledges crouched around in overcoats. Mum and Richard, being neat-handed, dealt with sausages and potatoes wrapped in foil. 'Hush,' said Dad to Laura. 'Be quiet and look. I think we've got a visitor.'

Low down, behind the flames, something moved and bright eyes glinted. Dad held out his hand, with a bit of sausage, and made the tshushing noise you do to cats. 'Puss?'

'Oh bother, it's gone again. I must have startled it, poor thing.'

But Laura didn't think she had seen anything like a cat. She had seen someone with hands, holding them out to the fire. When the bonfire supper was over, and she was supposed to be in bed, she crept down again and opened the back door. The embers of the fire glowed in the dark, the sausage and half a potato she'd left by the step were gone. 'Hello?' she whispered. 'Are you there? Why don't you come in? It's all over now. No one's going to hurt you.' But the boggart knew better. No one answered.

It was after bonfire night that the freezing weather really began. Now the Pledges found out what a Cauld House Moor winter would be like. Laura noticed that the ice on the puddles didn't melt all day at home, when it melted in her school playground by morning break.

And she thought the ice cracks in the poor old road were getting wider. Radiators and fires together were not enough to keep the house comfortable. The airing cupboard was empty of blankets, and the four of them stayed together in one room as much as possible. The Shores became very quiet and were never seen. One morning Mum went out with bread for the unhappy birds before driving to work, and found a message scratched on the wall by the kitchen door, as if with a stick of charcoal: GO AWAY! 'Stupid woman,' she said to herself, and rubbed it out.

Richard came down late to breakfast. It was a Saturday. It was terribly cold. He found Laura sitting reading the local paper. She had a car rug wrapped around her knees.

'You look like an old granny,' he said, which wasn't fair, as he himself was wearing his dressing-gown over his clothes, and a woolly hat to protect his ears. 'Have you been down to Cauld already?'

'No,' she said. 'Mum's been down and back, before she went to work. She went to try and make someone come and fix the boiler. You may have noticed – the heating is off.'

When the Pledges first moved into Cauld House they laughed because the house had storage radiators and central heating and open fires. They knew better now. Richard groaned.

'Where's the milk?'

'It's in the fridge to warm up.'

'Ho, ho, ho.'

'No, it's true. Everything that was left out had chunks of ice in it when we came down. So we switched off the fridge and put things in it. It's insulated.'

'Oh really? Could I sleep in there, d'you think?'

Laura had found something interesting in the *Cauld Moor and Sope Gazette*: 'Hey, look at this.'

'Cauld House Moor quake,' read Richard. 'Bus conductor makes a discovery. Mr Alfred Midfirth . . .'

'But he's the stationmaster.'

'Oh, they're always getting things mixed up. Read the rest.' Laura had unwrapped herself, and was climbing into her boots.

'Where are you off to?'

'I'm going to see the earthquake. Aren't you interested?'

'Not if it means going outside for longer than ten seconds.'

'But it's warmer outside.'

Richard laughed and complained, but she was right. There was a thick yellowish sky hanging low over the moor today, and the air had lost some of its knife-sharp edge. They should have been heading right down the hill to Cauld, but Laura dawdled and kept peering at the road surface. Just across the gully bridge, where the steep dry valley cut across the moor below the ridge, she stopped. She had found a crack.

'Look at this.'

'There are lots of cracks. This road is breaking up. It's the frost, and old age. Can we get on? It's not exactly warm, and have you noticed the sky?'

'But I think this crack is right in a line with the other ones. Remember how I led Edith and Tom about? We never looked *beyond* the house. I mean, they didn't and I didn't. Come on.'

She went plunging away, off the road and down the steep slope, as if she meant to jump on to the station roof, which was exactly below. There was nothing he could do but follow her. It was a hair-raising descent, especially because Laura kept stopping suddenly and peering at the ground again.

'Laura, what are we doing?'

'We're climbing down an invisible waterfall.'

With a final scramble she landed in a heap against the white painted palings of the station-yard, picked herself up and began to rattle at the wicket gate. Mr Midfirth opened it. He didn't seem surprised to see them. 'Ah,' he said. 'Come to have a look? Won't do you any good, you know.'

There was an eruption in Mr Midfirth's garden. The white fence enclosed a sloping piece of ground at the bottom of the hill. Mr Midfirth was proud of his garden. He had been tidying it and tending it even through this bitter frost. But it was ruined now. There had been a sort of landslide. The fence was uprooted for part of its length and the earth was broken up and thrown back as if someone inside the hill had been shoving their way out.

'Is that all?' demanded Laura.

'Aye,' said Mr Midfirth. 'No cups and no crowns. Stands to reason. Rivers don't stay in one place, over or under. Not in limestone, any road.'

'What *are* you talking about?' demanded Richard.

'In the book I lost,' said Laura, 'it said there was an underground river that might lead you to the treasure. Don't you remember?'

'Of course I do, that's how you tricked the Shores. But I thought it was a hoax.'

'It is,' said Laura. 'But not mine: Gertrude Carey's. I don't like our ancestor much. She let people get lost and killed, and she *knew* it was a red herring.'

'That's the Careys for you,' said Mr Midfirth. 'I didn't know you'd lost the book. That's a shame.'

93

'We're sorry,' said Richard.

'Oh no, lad,' said the stationmaster. 'It's your own property. Pity though. Eh, lad, I've done what I could. More than most people around here would allow. But look at this. And it'll get worse. Are you going to tackle her or aren't you? If you're not, say so, and I think we'd better all start packing. This is only the beginning, d'you see?' He peered into Richard's blank face and then, shaking his head, he gave up and began to point out the way the concrete of the platform was cracked as well.

'Water expands when frozen,' said Laura.

'It does that. And there's water all through this ridge. You can't see it, but we'll soon know about it if this goes on. I'm having some chaps from Manchester this afternoon,' he added, 'to look at the line. How d'you fancy walking to school, eh? And as I say this is only the beginning.'

Richard and Laura trudged back up the hill. 'But we did tackle her,' said Richard. 'That's what he must mean, isn't it? All his hints and so on. There must be some way of telling a witch, and he spotted Edith. He obviously reckons that living in that house and being descended from Careys we have to stop people going for the treasure. But we did. Wasn't the last thing we heard from next door something about being "finished with this place by Christmas"? So we've beaten them. We can't be expected to tackle the weather too.'

The snow began before they were half-way home. It poured down all afternoon. 'Pour' isn't usually a word you use for snow: snow drifts and floats and whirls. But this was a winter cloudburst, like a bucket emptying, as if no time must be wasted clearing the sky, so the bitter frost could grip again.

*

On the Monday of that week both Richard and Laura were kept out of school by the weather. The railway line was shut down while people checked that it was still safe. Laura's school had another heating crisis. They went out on the moor, taking the toboggan and an arctic picnic. As Laura said, it was no colder than indoors. But there were no real slopes except the gully, and there you'd only break your neck. In the end they found themselves at Richard's arena, where he'd seen Martian canals once, and a strange meeting. They sat on the toboggan. The snow was brilliant and lovely.

'I like this place,' said Richard thoughtfully. 'It has a nice feeling. It feels as if people have lived here.'

'Maybe they did,' said Laura. 'The Vikings could have lived here. Your canals could be the remains of something besides sheep pens. Why not? I tell you what,' she added, looking at the purple line of the Pennines, far away, 'our ancestor liked it too.'

'What?'

'This place. She painted that line of hills for the picture in her book. I'm sure it's the same. With that cone like a volcano in the middle, and our ridge with the boulder right in front of it. It's exactly the same as the place where they see Prince Karr with the ice princess, and they know she's not human because she leaves silver footprints in the grass. Just before she kills the first brother.'

A Viking village, a Norse legend – Richard got up from the toboggan and stood staring at the snowy landscape: 'Laura, tell me that story again.'

So Laura told, wondering what had upset him. A treasure. A thing, not really human. Where she walked, she left a trail of ice. Her touch was death. And finally she stayed to guard the treasure. To reach the Viking hoard you'd have to get past the guardian. Get past her, or somehow have her on your side.

'Richard? What's wrong?'

He remembered the day a lark sat and looked at something that wasn't human, and the breath of winter that crept into the August sunshine. He remembered the cold, cold feathers of a dead sparrow, and little Ally Shore standing in the snow saying 'I can't help it'.

'Laura! That story! It is true. It is happening now!'

She was bewildered. She said, 'But it's a myth and legend. It isn't real. You can tell by the way they talk.'

Richard couldn't explain himself. His head was filled with a jumble of ideas: Mr Midfirth was *frightened*. Something was loose on Cauld House Moor that could turn an underground stream into a fist of ice, that could break up roads and railway lines. The boggart wasn't afraid of the witch, but he's afraid of *someone*. Mr Midfirth said, 'Are you going to tackle her?' and he didn't mean Edith.

'What are we doing out in this snow?'

'I'm cold,' said Laura.

Richard was bundling away their foolish picnic. He started to snap 'So get moving' but he stopped. Kneeling in the snow, he turned his head. Something was coming towards them. They both felt it now, a flow of ice vapour cutting through the crisp and healthy air of the winter's day like a knife through butter. It was coming closer. They could see it. It picked up the powdery snow and carried it so you could see the shape of the moving air. The dancing white sparks gathered and formed an outline.

She didn't look at them. She wasn't interested, she was only out to play, in her element. Richard grabbed Laura and pushed her face down to her knees – he was afraid of what the breath of that thing might do. But it passed by. A few shocked seconds later they raised their heads. The white landscape was empty.

'Richard,' whispered Laura – her throat was very dry – 'did you see?'

'I saw,' he said. 'Not Edith. The other one. Laura, I think we just saw what Ally Shore looks like when – when she takes off her school uniform. Let's go home!'

But their adventures were not over yet. As they came to the road in sight of the house Richard gave a shout, and started to run. Laura was behind him. There was something at their gate, something like a brown animal. It was gone, of course, by the time they got there.

'Look,' said Richard. 'Footprints.'

There in the snow were the clear marks of small bare feet, quite human but with very splayed toes.

'Oh, why doesn't he come in?' said Laura. 'He's supposed to live in the house.'

'He's been warned off,' said Richard. 'We've just seen by whom. Can you blame him for being scared?'

'But Richard, in the stories, when you've beaten the witch the familiar can't do anything.'

The boggart had left something behind. It was skewered on a dead twig of the currant bush. It was a scrap of something like parchment or thin leather. There was one word scrawled on it. The boggart wanted to make a point very strongly – that was clear from the kind of ink he'd used. It had dried to a dirty reddish-brown in the cold parched air: FLEE!

8 Thin Ice

Laura was waiting for Richard at the High School gates. Laura wasn't supposed to travel into town on her own, but it had seemed the only way to arrange things. She was nervous. All the people milling around in uniform made her feel small and scrubby and, besides, she was afraid of seeing the thing that was on the moor, in its disguise again. At last Richard pounced on her: 'There you are! I was waiting round the other side. Come on, quickly. She'll be in her room. I asked her to wait.'

He saw her eyes flickering uneasily over the crowd and said, 'Oh, don't worry. Ally's away again. She's not going to jump out from anywhere.'

Dr Radleigh sat at her desk. Between her hands was the scrap of parchment with the boggart's desperate message. She listened to the whole story. A couple of times people knocked on the door, but she sent them away.

'So. You now believe that the spirit Alvilda in the legend and our Ally Shore are one and the same?'

'I don't know what I believe,' said Richard. 'But out there on the moor, in the snow, when Laura told me — she said the hills were the same — it all seemed to fit together. It was the wrong way up before. It's Dad's fault. If he had told us about Pledges and Careys properly before we'd have paid more attention. He's awfully absent-minded.'

'And also that amateur conjuror was having some effect on him,' murmured Dr Radleigh. 'Oh dear me!

And you are the heir of the family. And you were the one I asked to offer her the salt. Oh dear!'

Richard and Laura sat on the edges of their chairs, wondering what would come next. Dr Radleigh bent down and took something out of a drawer in her desk.

'Oh!' said Laura.

'Laura, is this the same as the book you lost?'

'Oh, yes it is! Where did you get it?'

'From a second-hand bookshop. It is no rarity. The shopkeeper said he'd seen several copies. Don't look so cast down. Examine it carefully.'

Laura picked it up. It had the same blue leather binding, the same writing on the spine and the front. She turned the pages slowly, first going straight to the back, and then leafing through the rest. Dr Radleigh waited. At last Laura said, 'No. I don't think it's the same. There was an extra page in the back of mine, saying it was special. A special one of just a few, only for the family.'

'Hmm. Anything else?'

'Well – I think so. It's these last pages, where the legend is. I'm sure in my book they were on nicer paper. It felt like pound notes. And it was clear, with wavery marks in it, like pound notes.' She hesitated, and added honestly: 'I'm not certain. I could be just imagining that I remember that.'

'Possibly. That's very interesting, Laura.'

Dr Radleigh took the book back, and put it aside with the boggart's message. 'Well, as you can see, I have been curious about your affair. I've been looking up the history of Cauld House Moor. Also, just a week or two ago I had the opportunity of speaking to Edith Shore. She didn't want to talk to me. I think she is getting nervous about the impression Ally makes in public, now

99

that winter is drawing on. But I had a good look at her. And when I realized that your neighbour is *not* a witch I did begin to wonder how she came to have a creature like Ally on hand. Yes.'

'But what are we going to *do* about it?'

Dr Radleigh frowned at Richard, took off her little gold glasses, looked at them, sighed, and put them on again. She folded her hands and propped her chin on her fingers and said:

'Nothing.'

The children stared. Dr Radleigh smiled apologetically. Richard and Laura looked at each other and got up to go. Clearly, the senior mistress had just been teasing them. She didn't believe a word of it.

'No, no,' said Dr Radleigh. 'Sit down. Listen to me: What is it Ally is accused of? Firstly, she is working for a nasty bullying woman who fancies herself a witch. But that is not proven. I don't see any connection between slow fear and wax, and an ice spirit. Events *could* be interpreted in Ally's favour, I said so at the time, remember. Secondly, she doesn't get on with one of the other long-time inhabitants of the moor.'

Dr Radleigh looked at the dramatic message, and shook her head again:

'An excitable and nervous little creature, who can't do the washing up without breaking one plate in three. A *notoriously* unreliable and touchy breed.'

'All right,' said Richard. 'I see what you mean. But what about the ice?'

'I was coming to that. Lastly, she is cold, and she makes her surroundings unnaturally and dangerously cold too. Now that could be serious, and I will certainly look into it. But Cauld House Moor has always had a reputation for bitter weather, without anything too disastrous occurring as a result. It could be that the ice sprite has an attraction for and an affinity with ice and snow without being able to cause or control them. Like a magnet and iron filings. Richard and Laura, I am going to ask you to be patient. From what you say Ally Shore seems to be getting tired of her human shape. It is quite likely that all she wants is to vanish again, to be free of the burden of the last few months. Like Ariel, you know. If her "coldness" is dangerous it is all the more important that we treat her with care. If we interfere, we may find ourselves helping the woman who called her up to hold her.'

'But what about the treasure?'

'Oh, yes, the treasure,' said Dr Radleigh. 'Is it in danger? Is it hidden where fingers of ice can seek it out, cracking open earth and stone? I wonder. But it is supposed to be guarded, you know. Perhaps it is quite safe. Now children. If you'll excuse me.'

She closed up her office, ushered them out of the school and drove them to the station. As he got out of the car Richard asked — he had been puzzling about this — 'Dr Radleigh? You didn't explain: How could *you* tell that Edith Shore wasn't a witch?'

Dr Radleigh just smiled, the way she used to smile when you couldn't see through an easy problem on the chess board.

'Think about it, Richard,' she said, and drove away.

Two weeks passed. Mr Midfirth's garden lost its sheets of shiny black polythene, and apart from the jumbled plants and a few patches of new cement the station was back to normal. A van came and took away some of the Shores' boxes, so it looked as if they really were moving out. The frost broke, and snow turned to sleet. When it seemed that Ally Shore had disappeared from Morrison High School – permanently, this time – Dr Radleigh asked Richard:

'How is life on the moor now? Getting easier?'

But Richard said, 'I don't know. We haven't seen *her*, and the underground glacier seems to have done its worst. But it isn't exactly comfortable.'

The Pledges were being persecuted by heating problems. It seemed as if not a day passed without something going wrong. Mysterious little 'power cuts' that had nothing to do with the electricity board (or at least they wouldn't admit it) plagued the house. It wasn't like the witchcraft. It didn't give you bad dreams, or make you peer over your shoulder and imagine things. But it was getting on everybody's nerves all the same.

'And I *still* feel as if someone's trying to push us out. I suppose that'll pass when the Shores have actually gone.'

Dr Radleigh said 'Hmm.' Later, Richard found himself called to her office. She had the first-year registers for the term. She was investigating Ally.

'I don't like your uneasiness,' she said. 'You are too closely connected with this creature for me to ignore your feelings.'

'Why d'you think she's staying away from school?'

'Oh, there is no mystery about that. In her own season, clearly the Shore woman's amateur magic can't hold her at all. She is becoming too much like herself. I still think she will soon return to her natural elements entirely, and leave us for ever. But let us look at her school record. Let's see if we can judge her. Sit down, Richard. I've nearly finished.'

Ally's cold company did not seem to have done much harm. Some children had had a good deal of time off, with colds and flu. Others seemed to thrive on Ally's presence. 'Bracing,' said Dr Radleigh. 'And a bit too bracing for some. It's just as one would expect. There is no evidence of . . .'

At that moment the door burst open, and in marched Mr Russell, the games teacher. He had Ally Shore with him; he was holding her by the scruff of her gym blouse. He looked furious. Dr Radleigh was so amazed to see Ally at all that she let him shout out his story without a word: someone had been frightened half to death.

'White as a sheet . . . and *cold* . . . The child's in severe shock . . . I don't know how this little monkey did it . . . or what she did.'

Richard could guess. Some kid had seen what he and Laura saw on the moor, but at closer quarters. Even now, to his eyes, the shape there in blouse and shorts looked strange, uncertain. He wondered how Mr Russell could bear to touch it.

Mr Russell had just noticed Richard. He was scowling, and wondering why Dr Radleigh didn't send the kid away. But Dr Radleigh said:

'Thank you, Mr Russell. I'll deal with the matter.'

The games teacher left, looking suspiciously at young Pledge, and wondering why his right hand suddenly felt numb, as if the blood had got cut off. When he had gone, the room was very still. The ice spirit and the elderly lady in her shabby old university gown stood looking at each other, measuring each other. There were no more disguises.

'Alvilda,' said Dr Radleigh, 'you cannot come here any more. I thought you understood that.'

She did not start at hearing her right name. She looked about the room. She looked at Richard, but he didn't meet her eyes. She shivered at the edges; there was a glitter on her hair and skin. Her mouth moved:

'I am staying.'

There was ice in the air. Richard had a vision of himself and Dr Radleigh being found in here rock solid, like sides of beef in a freezer. He wanted to jump up and fling the door open, but he didn't know if he could move. But it was nearly the end of term. So many things were going on. So many people wanted the senior mistress. The next second the phone was ringing, and someone was knocking at the door. The ice cracked, and the world was normal again.

'Come in,' said Dr Radleigh, perfectly calmly. Then three different people wanted her, and Richard was sent on an errand, and somehow Ally was out in the corridor as well. But the office door was ajar. She slipped inside again. She did not like to do this. For one thing she knew very well that her masquerade as a schoolgirl was wearing thin, and she had not wanted to come back to Morrison, not even for a day. But Edith Shore thought that Dr Radleigh was suspicious, and she wanted to do something about it. Ally, with no expression on her face, dipped her long white fingers into the pocket of Dr Radleigh's coat, which was hanging in a corner. A handkerchief came out, large and plain, with the initials 'DR' in a corner. It would do.

That evening – it was a Friday – the winter weather returned to Cauld House Moor. Richard and Laura sat playing scrabble by a huge log fire. White sleet spattered the windows. Mum said, 'Don't do that, you'll block the triple word.'

Laura dropped some letters, and muttered to Richard, 'And what then?'

'I don't know. Dr Radleigh went off, and she sent me

off too. I didn't get back to the office till after school, and she'd gone and her car had gone.'

'And the – Ally?'

'Gone too. Or – or not visible. I'm a bit worried, Laura. I don't think Dr Rad has the right idea about you know who.'

'What are you two muttering about down on the floor? Are we playing this game or not?'

It was a storybook evening, the kind of night the Pledges might well have sighed for when they lived on a city street. The wind howled over the desolate moor. Sleet turned to whirling snow. Mum got up and went to close the curtains at last. She stood at the window, her hands full of thick brown velvet folds, in front of the black, white-speckled glass. She stopped for a second. Was she looking at something outside? Only the snow. She came back to the fire, shivering:

'Brr. Antarctica starts at the edge of the rug.'

'Mum, did you see anything outside?'

'Only the snow,' she said, frowning. 'Only the snow, whirling into strange shapes.'

Richard and Laura glanced at each other, and quickly away. Dad came in from the kitchen. After several delays (there was something badly wrong with the oven) their shepherd's pie supper was ready.

'Shall we eat by the fire? Clear away the scrabble, Richard.'

Suddenly Dad stopped unloading his tray and said, 'Good Lord. There's someone at the door!'

In the middle of all the bluster of the storm was a different sharp-edged sound – someone rapping.

'It's the wind,' said Richard uneasily. He had been hearing that noise for a while, and trying to ignore it.

Mum said, 'It's only the letterbox flap.'

Ratatatat, said the storm, and made noises like a woman's voice, crying. Dad got to his feet.

'There *can't* be,' said Mum, and grabbed his arm.

The thing in the storm began to rattle and moan louder than ever. Laura jumped up and ran across the room. She had the bolts undone and was pulling at the doorknob before Mum grabbed her away. The wind yelled. A burst of hard snow pellets came flying into the room. Richard shouted and slammed his weight against the wood. The door was shut. Mum said, 'You see, Laura. There was no one there.'

She sounded bewildered, as if she was wondering why it had seemed so very important not to open the door. She looked at Richard: 'What did you mean?'

'Me?'

'When you slammed the door, you shouted "You can't come in!"'

It had stopped trying to get in now. It had raced off to dance on the roof and laugh at them. Richard didn't know what to answer, but just at that moment there was a yell from the fireside. It was Dad. He was kneeling on the rug looking amazed, dripping with meat and tomato sauce. The casserole was in pieces.

'Oh no! Our supper!'

He claimed he had been attacked: 'I was just putting it in the hearth to keep warm when there was a huge gust of wind down the chimney. And *something jumped into my arms*. Right into the mashed potato. I couldn't see anything, but – you heard it yell.'

'We heard *you* yell, you mean,' said Mum. 'What a story, Dick. You're worse than the children.'

When they had helped Dad to clear up the horrible mess they noticed that the huge gust of wind had somehow brought down snow with it. The fire was wet. It went out, and they could not revive it.

'That was a warning,' said Richard. He had come to Laura's room on his way to bed. 'That was her way of saying "Get out, or there's more where this came from."'

Laura huddled down under her covers, and didn't answer.

'Laura, why did you try and open the door? It was crazy.'

'I thought it was the boggart.'

'Did you really, Laur?'

'I thought it was. I had to let it in. I *had* to.'

Richard left her, feeling very worried.

When he was sure everyone would be asleep Richard got up again. He went quietly down to the kitchen. He poured a bowl of milk, took some bread and some cheese and laid them on a clean teacloth on the floor. He switched off the glaring electric light and lit a gentle candle. He said, to the empty room, 'Come on, boggart. We've no chance if we don't pull together.'

Nothing happened. Richard waited. Minutes passed. Something creaked in one of the cupboards under the sink.

'Ah,' said Richard.

Then something began to whisper. It was not the boggart. The voice came from nowhere and everywhere. It came from the wind that was still sighing outside. It came from the air. It said that the boggart had made a mistake; that the humans could not help him, or themselves, or be helped; that he had shut himself up in a stone box when the moor was his only home, his only hope. You cannot get out . . .

Richard did not hear the words. Perhaps there were no words. But he caught the drift.

'Don't listen!' he cried. 'It's a trick!'

Suddenly he realized that shadows were her allies. He jumped for the light switch, but as he jumped the candle fell on its side and something went scampering past him in the dark. He ran after. It was in the front room. He heard it scrabbling, and a rattle of fallen soot, and the ghost of a faint anguished wail: 'Sorry, sorry, sorry.'

'Oh no!' cried someone behind him. 'She'll kill it!'

It was Laura, wrapped in a blanket, at the bottom of the stairs.

'I wouldn't worry about the boggart if I were you,' said Richard. 'It is safe enough on the moor, I think. It's ourselves we should be worrying about. We've got to get away from this house!'

9   The Blizzard

That weekend was an arctic ordeal. Something was wrong with the central-heating boiler again. The oven wouldn't get hot. They dragged out, not for the first time, Cauld House's formidable array of electric fires, antique and modern. But the lights kept going dim, and the bars of the fires stayed dull and cold. 'It's almost as if something close is draining the power,' said Mum. 'D'you think those Shores are secretly running a particle accelerator?'

It was Sunday afternoon. Mum was composing Christmas shopping lists. Dad and Laura were at Dad's school's Christmas party. Mum sat writing lists of how many boxes of dates and how many bananas, and when to collect the turkey. Her fingers were stiff with cold. She was sitting at the kitchen table in a fur jacket and still shivering. 'We put it in at lunchtime on Christmas Eve, (but I'll be home by then). That is, if the oven can raise itself above twenty degrees centigrade.'

Suddenly she broke off, exclaimed, 'I can't stand this!' and threw her pen at the wall. She buried her head in her arms. Richard looked at her anxiously. Was she crying?

'Mum?'

She lifted her head. 'Richard, fetch me the phone book. Get me the number of a fancy hotel. The Rutland will do. Richard, I can't bear to spend Christmas in this horrible house, on this horrible moor. It isn't fun living in the arctic if your igloo has no heat or light. And what is the point of hoarding money in this day and age? No discussions. No conferences. Give me that phone book!'

Richard and Laura were extremely relieved. They did not worry about what would happen after Christmas. The Shores would be gone, they would have done what ever they came to Cauld to do. Perhaps they'd get away with the 'treasure'; perhaps Ally would turn on them at the last moment; perhaps they would find out at last that the treasure didn't exist. 'Whatever it is,' said Richard, 'that's going to happen, we'll be out of its way. That is the important thing.' Laura had to agree. Everyone was happy. The laughter and the cheerfulness of that Sunday night made you realize, Richard thought, what a gloom had been gathering before. A horrible feeling of impending doom. But it was over now. He would have told Dr Radleigh about the new plan, but he couldn't. Dr Radleigh wasn't at school on Monday.

Dad's term was nearly over. Mum said she'd commute from the Rutland – it was the city's finest hotel – until Christmas Eve. Meanwhile, the central-heating firm and the electricians could move into Number One Cauld House and sort it out. 'I'm not giving up on your ancestral home, Dick,' she said to Dad. 'We'll come back.' On the twentieth of December there was a big schools' carol concert at the cathedral. Hordes of children from miles around would be turning up in coaches and buses and minibuses. The Pledges would all be there but Mum, and she would join them in the evening at the hotel. On the night of the nineteenth Number One was packed up. Richard saw a curtain twitch, next door, as he carried a big bag of interesting parcels out to the car.

'Well,' he thought. 'You've won.'

*

The next morning Richard was the last to leave. In the little pile of Christmas cards that the postman handed to him there was a letter, addressed to him. This was very unusual. Richard turned it over, trying to recognize the handwriting.

'You're all off, are you?' said the postman. 'Can't say I blame you. Bit parky for the festive season up here. It's all very well on the cards, isn't it?'

He was not a local man. He did the whole area in a van. He gave Richard a lift into Cauld, and then Richard had to drop in at the electrician's house so he nearly missed the train. It wasn't until he was at school, sitting waiting to be marshalled off to the cathedral, that he opened the mail. A card from an Australian aunt. A card from one of Dad's parents. A letter, addressed in strange but familiar writing:

Dear Richard,

First of all, a general apology. I have a strong reluctance for involving outsiders, especially young people, in a certain neglected branch of the natural sciences.

In this case I was mistaken, and so we are now in difficulties. Ally gave herself away, didn't she, that afternoon in my office? She means to *stay*. We cannot let her, I'm afraid.

I am ashamed to say that the truth about Ally was staring me in the face in those registers, but somehow I did not see it. Do you remember the startling cold at the end of September? And the freak snow, just a month later? Ally disappeared from school the day after that snowfall, and did not return until several days later. But she was able to appear and go about quite normally then, until the period of your experience on the moor. When I saw her still able to appear a schoolgirl in *December* that afternoon when we were discussing the registers, I finally realized what sort of creature Ally is. We have been calling her 'the witch's familiar' and 'the guardian of the treasure'. I had assumed that your distant ancestor, the Norseman, was the original magician who conjured her out of the ice and snow. This is a common, though regrettable, practice in magic. The 'thing' involved is most properly regarded as a kind of robot. It has no will, except for a faint consciousness that it is being used, and a desire to escape. Eventually, and especially in unskilled hands, it fades away into its original element, such as wind, water – snow. But Ally is *not* one of these. She is a true elemental; the test of this is that she waxes and wanes with the moon. I blame your ancestress, Richard. If she had not dressed up the legend of 'Prince Karr' in such fanciful language and costume, I might have guessed the truth sooner. But I am sure she had her reasons. There might even be such fools in the world. I mean people might have realized the 'value' of a force like Ally's.

Here, then, is our position. Alvilda is immortal. She is ice and snow. When she gives up her guardianship of the treasure the bones of the earth will crack and break. It is not a question of saving your family heirlooms, Richard. Far more is at stake. I do not like to think how much. Worse still, this week the winter solstice coincides with a full moon. I feel sure that *this* is the date your reckless neighbours will choose for their robbery, for Ally's power will be at its strongest, even handicapped as she is. They cannot have the slighest conception of what they are about to let loose on the world. Excuse my abrupt style, I am about to leave the city to consult with my superiors. I will return on the twentieth without fail. I will come straight to Cauld House. I must be there on the night of the full moon. And either you or your father must be with me. Our best hope, you must realize, is in your name. Your ancestress was a fine magician. She would not have exacted such a promise if it was worthless.

The day of the cathedral concert is a half day, of course. I will meet you and young Laura at Cauld House. Get away from the carols as quickly as possible. I'll be waiting for you. Good luck.

Dorothea Radleigh.

The last paragraph was written very scratchily, as if by someone in a great hurry. 'Why is Ally handicapped?' thought Richard. 'And what's that about my name?' He stuffed the letter in his pocket, and wondered how on earth he was going to get Dad back to Cauld House now. He could hardly show his father this letter.

So here he was on the cathedral steps. Children were pouring out of buses. The local radio station was trailing wires about, people were stamping their feet and rubbing their frosted noses. He saw his father, helping kids out of the special school's bus. He saw Laura and dived towards her through the crowd. Minutes later he was hurrying her through the streets, where Christmas shoppers were just beginning to appear, and explaining breathlessly.

'But what about Mum and Dad?' Laura asked.

'I told my class teacher,' said Richard, 'that if my Dad is looking for me and you afterwards, we've gone straight home to Cauld. He won't know what is going on, but he'll have to come after us. After that, it's up to Dr Radleigh.'

'We'll get in a row for missing the carols.'

'No, we won't. We'll get made life peers for saving the world from an ice age. Get the tickets. I'll see when's the next train.'

Shivering, they stood on the doorstep of Cauld House. The snow lay all around, and the sky was ominously dark. There was a very penetrating wind.

'O-open up!' said Laura, through chattering teeth.

But Richard couldn't. Their front door had an ordinary Yale lock, and another more formidable lock that was hardly ever used. Because they were going away, Richard had locked both behind him an hour or two ago. But he had left his keys at the electrician's. Laura only had a Yale key.

'Oh no!'

'Have you got a bit of plastic? We could try that James Bond thing.'

'No I haven't. And that wouldn't work with the mortise. We'll have to wait for Dad.'

'We'll freeze to death.'

Then Richard remembered the kitchen window catches. It was when they were prising and struggling round at the back that they noticed, over the snowy wall, movement and voices from inside Number Three. Somebody opened a window.

*

The parlour of Number Three was emptier, this morning, than it was the day Richard saw it. All the packing-cases had gone, and most of the furniture. In a corner stood Tom and Edith's luggage, and a couple of new, empty cases, reinforced to carry articles that would be very heavy. Tom was engaged in scraping the leather of these, so they didn't look so new. Edith was busy too. She was on her hands and knees by the hearth. She had a paper bag full of clean wood ash, and a small bottle of oil. She was mixing the two together into a sort of putty on a marble pastry slab. The third person in the room looked on, bored and amused. Ally had grown since her last day at school. She was a woman now, made of something clear and hard and substanceless like glass. It was not ice. It was a good deal colder than frozen water. Tom got up and opened a window. The air outside was comparatively warm. Then he went to switch on a light because the snow clouds made such a gloom.

'No,' said Edith. 'That won't work now.'

She had finished modelling her putty. It was meant to be a three-dimensional sketch of the road outside, from Cauld House down to beyond the dry gully. There was a dangerous blind bend, just before the bridge.

'Is this going to kill that teacher?' asked Tom, peering at the mess.

'It's her own fault,' said Edith. 'If she doesn't come up the road, nothing will happen to her.'

'That's fair enough,' said Tom. 'And there'll be nothing to show it's not an ordinary road accident?'

'Nothing. Now I just take her handkerchief.'

Edith cut a small ragged strip from the handkerchief, using a knife, not scissors, the way the book said. She tied it in the special knot, and laid it down, carefully, on the ash and oil road.

'Something in her way,' she explained. 'Just something to make her swerve. The oil for a skid, the ash in her eyes. And then the gully. I'm really getting the hang of adapting these old recipes.'

Tom grunted. 'I get you. Sounds all right to me.' But he looked behind him uneasily. He thought he felt watched: 'Hey!' With a jump and a yell he flung the first thing that came to hand at the open window. Edith turned on him.

'What's got into you?'

'There's somebody out there! That little sneak again!'

Edith's voice came through the open window. Tom was to sit down and shut up. He wasn't the only one whose nerves were on edge. The children crept back from where they had ducked under the snowy bushes.

'Why, it's my book!' whispered Laura, picking up Tom's missile.

But Richard didn't care. 'Don't worry about that now,' he gasped. 'Didn't you hear? Dr Radleigh's probably on that road now. We've got to warn her!'

Gertrude Carey's book was left in the front porch. The children set off at a swift jog-trot down the icy road to Cauld.

In Number Three Tom and Edith went on rubbing down their suitcases and going over their travel plans. The Winter Daughter sat by the long-dead fire, and looked at the amateur little device of Edith's magic. She sighed, and the air cracked like crystal. She leaned forward and took a strand of her hair, or was it a handful of the glitter of her skin, and tossed it down on Edith's sticky model. The icy sparks fell, and as they fell, the space between them and the grey mound on the slab seemed to grow enormous. A whisper of white, falling, falling. The crude map changed. There, in tiny relief, was the house, the upland flowing evenly away below until it was cut by a narrow gorge. The trees in the gorge were quite clear – birch trees with thin trunks like split matchsticks. And the road, winding up to the little doll's-house bridge, a strip of dark grey in the featureless snow. Far away down the miniature road there were two points of light – sidelights for a heavy, threatening winter gloom. There came the sound of an engine, tiny and far, far away. The glimmering sparks fell through the air and touched something that was lying on the road. Then that white scrap of fabric wavered, stirred and seemed to take on a shape, the shape of a small human figure. There was a child on the road.

'Wait, wait,' gasped Richard. 'This is no good. Don't you realize? Whatever Edith's done we're going to run straight into it!'

They stopped, breathing hard, and stared around. The house was just out of sight behind, there was nothing visible but the strip of grey tarmac, and a blue shadowed expanse of white creaming away on every hand. The sky was very low. They were two black matchstick figures in a blank arctic landscape, like ants on a piece of paper. They felt helpless and desperate. One look at the clouds told them it wasn't only Edith's magic they had to fear. At last Richard cried 'This way!' and sprang off the road to the right.

They were running for the dry valley. Above the bridge it was more uneven. There were boulders and small birch trees growing in it, and the climb down and up would not be too difficult. They could both see the tops of the trees on the skyline every time they came up a rise, spidery blue black figures on an ochre sky, so they couldn't get lost. Their feet crunched the crusted snow. There was no hope of finding a footpath, they just jogged on.

The beginning of the snow caught them in a dip between two vast white waves. It came with a rush, and the wind came plunging after. In seconds they were surrounded. It might as well have been midnight. The whole landscape disappeared in a snow-white whirl.

'I knew we shouldn't have left the road! Stop, Richard. Stop!'

'Keep going, keep going . . .' He thought she was right, but it was no use trying to find the road now. Their only hope was to keep straight on.

'No, Richard! We're lost. Where are the trees? Richard, I think we've turned right round. We just came up this bit.'

'No, we're not. Hold my hand.'

'Let's wait until it passes.'

They stopped in the shelter of the last slope they had come down, and crouched together. But the snow squall showed no signs of easing. Richard insisted on starting off again.

'If we keep straight on we must hit the gully. We can follow it to the bridge.'

They got to their feet and began to march forward, hand in hand. They tried to keep steady, but the wind seemed to come from all directions at once. Then Richard realized that however hard he tried to march straight on Laura, at his left, was tugging him to the left, to the road. He was certain that this was wrong.

'Don't, Laura. We've got to stick to one idea. We'll never find the road now. The gully's our best bet.'

'I want to go back.'

'Laura, you can't. We can't separate.'

She twisted her hand, trying to get free. The snow flung itself in their faces and the wind made them stagger.

'No! Laura!' shouted Richard.

'It's the magic!' she shouted back. 'It's the magic, making us get lost. *Let go of me.*'

With a final vicious wrench she was free, and sprinting away from him over the snow.

'No!' yelled Richard. He dashed after her. There was nothing else he could do.

Richard was lost. The wind had died down. Now there was only the snow, falling and falling. It was inside his clothes, it was inside his boots. It seemed as if it was inside his eyes too, and dancing around in his head. Every so often he called 'Laura', but he knew she wasn't going to answer. After a while he sat down on a white lump. The house could not be far away. The road could not be far away. But he had no sense of place. He did not know which way he had come. He couldn't even follow his own footprints, the new snow had already swallowed them up. He thought now that Laura had been quite right. What made me leave the road and run on to the moor in the first place? Why wouldn't I turn back? Magic! He sat on the lump and called 'Laura?' There was no sound in the snow hush. He wondered what the magic would do to him next, but he was too tired to worry about it. His arms and legs seemed to be stiffening up as if he had been running for hours. The snow patted on his cheeks. He shook his head like a horse shaking off flies, but the snow wouldn't go away. He thought, 'I'll close my eyes. If only it would stop dancing, I'd get my bearings.' He closed his eyes.

*

There was a house in front of him. It was built partly of wood and partly of packed stones. There were smaller houses around it. There were people moving about clearing the snow from in front of their doors, tossing out rubbish for the snow to bury. They were dressed in thick, dirty-looking woollen clothes, long shirts and leggings. Richard blinked – for a moment he glimpsed the 'Martian canals'. They were ditches under the embankments that the huts were built on. The stones of the walls were tumbled; some of them had been used to make rough sheep pens. The two different pictures, of the same place, struggled in his eyes. He shook his head; a man came out from somewhere. He was limping. One of his legs was weak and crooked, it looked as if it had always been that way. *They are a hard people – deformed or sickly babies have to bear the snow, to prove themselves.* The limping man was standing in front of Richard. His face was sad. He spoke. But Richard did not understand his language. The man seemed to realize this. He bent down and seemed to pick something off the ground. Then he stood up again. He tried to take Richard's hand, but Richard didn't feel anything touching him . . .

There was nothing but the snow and the moor. Richard stood up. Of course he knew where he was. He was in that place with the sheep pens and the Martian canals. He recognized the lumps and bumps, even shrouded in snow. *What happened? Did I close my eyes for a second?* You should never do that in the snow. It's very dangerous. There was something in his hand. His fingers had closed over it automatically as he stood up; he could feel that it was a twig, or something like. He had a sharp, brief feeling that someone had just tried to tell him something important, but there was no time for that now. He remembered what danger Dr Radleigh must be in, and that Laura would be trying to find her. She would be heading for the bridge. He thrust whatever it was into his pocket, and away he ran. There was no trouble in finding his way. Soon he could feel the surface of the road through the snow underfoot. He turned downhill and ran like the wind.

When Laura dashed away from her brother she wasn't being reckless. She just thought it was the only way to stop him leading them out into the storm until they died of exposure. But it was terribly easy to lose all sense of direction. She ran, found that Richard wasn't following her, and, fatally, turned back. She could not find him. She could not hear him. She could not even trace her own footprints. Finally, she stumbled over what seemed to be just another shadow, and then she was falling, tumbling head over heels down a steep and endless-seeming slope.

The next thing she knew, she was lying in darkness, with a cold weight on top of her. She kicked out in panic and the pile of soft snow fell away. The dark was replaced by a whitish gloom. There was snow melting in her ears and shivering down her spine, but she wasn't hurt. She looked up at the white sides of the valley, and the ghost bodies of the birches. She and Richard had run further than they'd thought. This was the gully already. She had been very lucky not to crash into a boulder or a tree.

'Richard!' she shouted. 'I'm in the valley!'

But there was no answer, only an echo. Laura began to be very frightened indeed. 'Richard! Richard!' she cried. It was certain that he must have been close behind her, or somewhere near her. Why didn't he answer? He must have fallen too.

'Oh! Help.'

There was no daylight. She could make out nothing in this pale, blind gloom. She did not know how to begin searching. She scrambled to her feet. She had one idea: to get back to the house, to find Dad, to find Dr Radleigh. Still calling 'Richard!' 'Richard!' in a thin frightened voice, she started to struggle up the side of the gully to the road bridge.

Dr Radleigh was in a bad temper. She had stopped in Cauld, to try to find out if the Pledge children had come home from town. But the station-yard was chained up. There was a message on a blackboard: 'Line Closed Due To Adverse Weather Conditions.' The stationmaster, who had just finished writing this, saw someone looking inquisitive, and hurried out of sight. The supermarket was shut. A street of blank windows, and slyly twitching curtains. Dr Radleigh drove on.

She was not surprised to meet the blizzard. When the snowfall began she smiled grimly, stopped the car, and took the tyre chains out of the boot. She had borrowed them from a friend who used to go skiing in Scotland. When she'd finished the job she stood up and looked at the moor. The snow was not heavy yet, down here. She stepped a few paces over the tussocky ground, patched in black and white, until she could look up the flank of the hill. There was the storm, wrapped around Cauld House, thick as a moving cloud, bright as sugar icing. It looked like a churning waterspout, between a white sea and a yellow sky.

'Hmm,' said Dr Radleigh. She calculated that she would be driving into that little patch of trouble just at the steepest part of the hill. The children would be alarmed if they were home now. They wouldn't know how local the storm was – as yet. She turned back to the car, exclaimed 'Hey!' and started to run. But it was no good. The thing she'd seen crouched by her front wheel was gone again.

What did he want? A lift? Silly creature.

Then she saw that there was a bunch of thorny bramble thrust into her near front tyre. She dragged it away – the thorns were horrendous.

'Whose side are you supposed to be on?' muttered Dr Radleigh, indignantly. But no one answered. The nervous little brown person had vanished again, into the snowy moorland.

Dr Radleigh's car took the steep bends before the bridge on three tyres and a slow puncture. It wasn't Dr Radleigh's fault she was going so slowly. She was pumping the accelerator. It had occurred to her that the storm around Cauld House now must mean that something was happening already, and the children were probably there alone. She came around the last worst corner . . .

'What?'

It was hopeless. There was someone in the road. There was a child in the road. She seemed to pop up out of nowhere – a white face. The car swerved wildly. A handful of snowflakes slapped the windscreen and Dr Radleigh flinched. She recovered, but the car could not. It careered over the bridge, left the road and, with a groan and a screech of torn metal, it rammed itself into the side of the hill. There was a long sighing whisper of new snow broken up, and then there was silence.

10   *The White Solstice*

Richard stopped running when he heard and saw the crash. There was Laura, standing in the middle of the road.

'I thought you were buried,' she said dazedly.

Snowflakes were already misting over the tracks where Dr Radleigh had gone off the road. The wind had dropped. The blizzard had vanished. It was impossible to believe that even two children could have lost themselves or been afraid in this quiet landscape. A little snow, a little wind – what is so awesome about that? Richard had the feeling that someone was laughing at them. He knew he would have to go to the crashed car and look inside, but the thought of what he might find was too horrible.

Then slowly and protestingly the passenger door began to open. Laura gasped. Two rather long thin feet, in sensible walking shoes, appeared. Dr Radleigh sat half out of the car, rescuing her spectacles from one ear, and putting them back on her nose. There was a cut across her forehead.

'Well,' she said drily. 'It is lucky I did not need your first aid. Speed is most important. Are we going to stand here all day?'

As she spoke something moved behind them, up on the ridge. It was exactly as if a cat had let go of a mouse that was playing dead. The cat had been crouched back, watching them, hoping for more play. Now she pounced. Dr Radleigh jumped to her feet and grabbed Richard and Laura's arms. At the same moment a great white paw of snow and wind came rushing down the hill and snatched away everything in sight.

They fought their way up the hill with their heads down, Dr Radleigh between the children.

'Made it!' cried Laura, as they fell into the shelter of the porch. The snow dashed by the entrance, but none came in.

'No,' said Dr Radleigh. 'We were allowed to reach the house. We are needed, or at least Richard is needed, that is why. What is the trouble now, Richard?'

Of course they were still locked out. They had forgotten all about that. This time there was no question of carefully forcing a window catch. It seemed stupid to risk even a few more yards around the house. Supposing Ally changed her mind? Richard took a half brick that had been used for scraping shoes, and ducked out into the garden. He scrambled on to the porch roof. He was soaked and freezing. He crouched there on the gable, expecting some wicked twist of the wind to snatch him off and throw him down, but nothing happened. The wind dropped to a listening hush.

'Cat and mouse,' said Richard to himself. He pushed aside the softly crusted fresh snow, and read, as he had read once before, 'QUIS CUSTODIET IPSOS CUSTODES?' – Who guards the guards? 'It's all there, the whole secret. The guardian far more dangerous than what she guards is valuable . . . the family pledged to keep *her* safe, not the crown jewels.'

He wondered what had happened to the boggart.

'Richard? What are you doing up there?'

He was getting very cold and uncomfortable. He leaned out, and swung with his brick against Laura's bedroom window.

The house felt cold and dead, as if it had been empty

for months. Dr Radleigh took charge. She didn't seem surprised to hear they had problems with electricity. She advised them not to depend on it for light or for heat at all. There was a paraffin fire under the stairs, never used because of the evil smell. This was fetched out, and two paraffin lanterns as well. She made the children change their wet clothes and bring them downstairs, with heaps of rugs and blankets. The clothes were set to dry, Laura was told to roll up blankets and pack them under the door sill and round the windows.

'We must stay together, in one room. We must conserve heat as much as possible. Is there any more fuel besides this can?'

'There might be some in the garage. Or in the coal shed, with the logs.'

'Better not risk it.'

'It's only a few yards – I'll go.'

'No, Richard. None of us must be alone from now on. It isn't only the weather we have to fear.'

She was sitting on the couch, wet clothes steaming on chairbacks all around her. Richard noticed that she was very pale. The gash on her forehead was not bleeding, but an ugly bruise was gathering round it. She did not look well. In her hands was the book, Gertrude Carey's book.

'It is an advantage that you have this book again. Not much of an advantage, but something. There were three. Your neighbours must have had one copy from the beginning; what happened to the missing one, the one your father's family lost, I suppose, we'll never know. I have been speaking to a specialist about the watermark magic. The main purpose of this book, three times over, in case of loss or accidents, is the control of the ice spirit. The power is hidden within the retold legend. We will do what we can with it.'

Laura finished her job, and came to the couch in time to see Dr Radleigh carefully pulling the precious heirloom apart. She was detaching the last pages, the legend, from the rest of the book.

'I am sorry, Laura. I have to do this. It releases – '

'The safety catch?'

'Exactly. Let me explain. When we first discussed Ally, I was convinced that the Shores were no danger to anyone except themselves. They had managed to conjure the ice spirit, but whatever they believed in the end the "guardian" must be true to her task, having no mind of her own. Ally wasn't helping Edith; she had no part in your original troubles. I believed that in the end she would deal with the thieves, and we had better not interfere. But now we know that Ally has decided to betray her trust. The way to the treasure is through this house, that is obvious. Show me this cellar of yours now.'

To their surprise Dr Radleigh did not tap the walls, or peer at the floor. She simply stood at the bottom of the wooden steps, with Richard holding up a paraffin lamp behind her, and read aloud, steadily but quietly, some paragraphs from the story of Prince Karr. Laura stared into the gloom, but no magic door appeared. Dr Radleigh turned round and climbed the steps again, leaning heavily on the rail.

'What did you do? What was that for?'

Dr Radleigh sat down at the kitchen table. The room was full of a pale, shadowy snow light. The clock on the wall said it was just past noon. She said:

'To make it less easy for her to enter, or the thieves.

It will not last long, it will not help much. They'll get past you one way or another. That is inevitable.'

Richard was shocked: 'But I thought you said the spell controls Ally?'

'That is true. What remains in these pages will control her. But it cannot be done by force. It has to be accepted.'

'What on earth do you mean? Ally's not going to accept anything! It's impossible!'

He forgot who he was speaking to, he was so shocked to hear her calmly saying – in so many words – that there was no hope at all. The senior mistress smiled as he became confused at having been so rude to her.

'There is some hope,' she said. 'But it depends on *you*, Richard.'

Laura stared at her brother. 'On *Richard*?' She couldn't believe it. The kitchen clock ticked. Richard was trying to remember something, something that made sense, in a strange way, of what Dr Radleigh was saying. There was something he wanted to ask her about, something that had happened recently. But there were too many events – the car crash and the blizzard, and now the beginning of a siege. Dr Radleigh had fallen silent. She was looking fixedly at the table top. Suddenly she raised her head and said:

'Richard! Laura! Where are your parents? Why aren't they here?'

'Well, Mum's at work,' said Richard. 'But Dad should be coming back. I left a message with my teacher we were coming back here, so he'd have to follow. I couldn't tell him about Ally. I thought I'd leave that to you. But I'm a bit worried. He's on a bike, he might not be able to get out here in the snow . . .'

He broke off. Dr Radleigh wasn't listening. She was

staring vaguely. Her lips moved: 'Snow . . . snow,' she murmured, and then, very gently, she began to keel over forwards, falling from her chair. It happened so slowly Richard and Laura seemed to be watching for several minutes, unable to move.

'What's happened to her?' breathed Laura. 'Is it more magic?'

'I don't think so. I think it's concussion.'

They managed to get Dr Radleigh to her feet and into the living-room, but there she collapsed completely.

'Phone for an ambulance,' said Richard, putting rugs over her. He couldn't remember what you were supposed to do about concussion. Were you supposed to keep the person awake?

Laura was staring. 'Well – phone, can't you?'

'I'll try,' said Laura. But she was not surprised to find she only heard a faint thin buzzing. She dialled Cauld railway station instead, and for a moment she got through:

'Mr Midfirth? Is that you? Listen, I'm at Cauld House. There's only me and Richard. We're in trouble. We need help . . .'

Richard was trying to open Dr Radleigh's fingers, that had closed tightly over the pages secretly written with Gertrude Carey's spell – the only weapon they had. He could not free the paper without tearing it.

'I wouldn't do it right probably, anyway. What do I know about magic? You'd better just wake up, Dr Radleigh. Better still, let's all wake up, and find this was just a bad dream.'

He put the hand under the blanket, and looked round to find Laura peering into the telephone receiver and shaking it.

'What's wrong?'

'It's gone. It was Mr Midfirth. I heard him cough. But we were cut off.'

'Dial again.'

But the phone was dead.

'Of course,' said Richard. 'The lines will be down because of the storm.'

Laura said: 'Yes. Because of the storm. Did you really think they would let us phone for help? They've got us trapped.'

The paraffin fire was keeping the room warm, at least. Their outdoor clothes steamed. Dr Radleigh lay unconscious. Her face was ash-coloured and her eyes were not properly closed, but she was breathing evenly, and there was nothing they could do for her, but keep her wrapped up and watch. Richard made an expedition to the kitchen and came back with biscuits, cocoa, milk, sugar – a saucepan. He made a camp and began to heat milk over the chimney of the paraffin heater.

'If Dad doesn't come soon,' he said cheerfully, 'I'll go out hunting again and kill a tin of tuna fish and drag it back here.'

But Laura stood at the window. The snow crowded at the glass, plastering it up so the faint daylight could hardly struggle through. Richard came over. They saw something moving out at the garden gate – a humped figure in boots and anorak, peering up the path – Tom. It moved away.

'Polar bears,' said Richard.

There was nothing left beyond the shrouded garden but snow, snow, snow.

'The road's gone,' said Laura.

Richard made her leave the window. He shut the

curtains. The room instantly filled with a deep under-water gloom, but they only lit one lamp, not two. 'We are saving fuel,' thought Laura. 'We both know very well no one can get to us now.'

Richard poured hot milk and sat sipping his cocoa. He was soon lost in thought: the White Solstice. Dr Radleigh had been preparing for an attack, but what kind of an attack? What were they waiting for? He wondered if he should try to find a diary or an almanac that would tell him the time of the moonrise. He did not even know the time of sunset, but he realized unhappily that it was certainly only a few hours away by now. What would they do? What if they couldn't find the treasure anyway? Would they tear the house apart, like a glacier tearing a mountain?

Laura began to hear noises. It was the sighing wind in the big old chimney, but it was not sighing. It was scratching. Scratch, scratch, like a rat. She looked at Richard, but he was just gazing at his cocoa, in a dream, not hearing anything.

Scritch, scrabble.

There was something there, up inside the wall. Richard could not hear it. She looked at his blank face and suddenly felt, with a shudder, that she was alone again, hearing things that nobody else heard, thinking things that nobody believed. She remembered the first blizzard and how the snow came down the chimney, like a probing finger. It killed the fire, but the fire was there at least. There was nothing in the hearth now.

'Laura!'

Richard almost dropped his mug. Laura had suddenly, without a word, jumped to her feet and started dragging at the handle of the paraffin fire. She was trying to heave it across to the hearth, still lit!

'Laura! Are you crazy? What's got into you? Let go of that!'

'I can't, I can't. I've got to put it under the chimney. She's coming down the chimney. Like the wolf . . .'

She wouldn't let go. When he jumped up and tried to stop her she stared at him as if he was an enemy, and fought furiously. They tussled. Richard got her hands off the handle, but she kicked and struggled so much that they both landed on the floor, dangerously near the fire and the lamp.

'Listen, listen!' cried Laura. Someone's foot kicked and the lamp went over. Luckily it went out straight-away. Richard gave a gasp of relief, but at the same moment Laura *screamed*. Something had landed with a thump in the grate. As they lay paralysed with startled fright there was a further scrabbling and it *ran over them*. They felt its feet and hands.

It was gone, somewhere in the room. Laura and Richard sat up cautiously. Nothing happened. Richard reached out a slow hand for the lamp and the matches.

'Where is it?'

The lamp flame suddenly showed them each other's pale faces, and a shadowy room that looked vast, full of hiding places. Something moved. One of the heavy curtains stirred, near the floor.

'Come out,' said Richard. 'Let us see you.'

The boggart came out. They saw a creature about three feet high, dressed in leather the same colour as its horny brown skin. It had a shock of ragged dark hair, huge eyes that seemed to be lidless, like a snake's – and no chin to speak of. Melted snow dripped from it on to the carpet. It was shivering all over its skin, like a dog.

'Humphrey!' said Laura.

The boggart didn't waste any time on the children.

Once he was sure they weren't going to do him any harm he made straight for the couch where Dr Radleigh lay. Apparently he didn't realize at first that she was unconscious. It seemed as if he had a great respect for her. He stopped at the foot of the couch and made a sort of bow, with his hands over his face. When nothing happened he peeped through his fingers. He crept closer, and peered, and sniffed. When he had satisfied himself that she really was sick and helpless he said, in a small, rough voice:

'Oooh. The strong one is down already. Not good.'

He made a quick, shifty movement, back to the chimney probably. But Richard grabbed his skinny little arm.

'Oh no, you don't! I see. You thought you'd join us because you saw we had help. And now you find we're helpless you're off again. *Quis custodiet* is right, and not just about Ally. You should be ashamed of yourself. Anyway, I'm not letting you go.'

The boggart wriggled and showed his sharp teeth, but when he realized Richard was determined he began to cry instead. He wept that he 'always helped . . . I always help . . . But I am so small, I can only do small things. I try to help this one, I make her car go slow . . . I do my best.'

When they worked out that he had been on the road and could have warned their friend, but had played a trick on her instead, they were horrified.

'Some help you are!'

The boggart snivelled that he was afraid to talk to magicians, strangers, and he did not like motor cars.

'What's that got to do with anything?'

'There's no point in shouting at him, Laura. All right,

boggart. You did your best. Can you do anything for her now?'

The boggart crouched down and very cautiously put a dirty small hand on Dr Radleigh's face. When he took his fingers away, she was certainly a better colour, and her breath began to be slow and steadier.

'She's asleep. Oh thank goodness!'

The boggart sniffed. Laura said 'I'm sorry I snapped' and offered him a blanket. He gave another self-righteous sniff and trailed with the blanket over to the paraffin fire, where he squatted down and began doing things to the wick. The flame became bluer and clearer. Laura and Richard sat down by him. He hunched his shoulders and wouldn't look up.

'Humphrey, we're sorry. We really need your help. You're the only one who can tell us about Ally, and what is going to happen.'

The boggart sniffed again: 'That Humphrey? Is that a name for me?'

'Well, yes. We didn't know any other.'

'Got none,' said the boggart. 'Only *that dratted*. Only once had a name. Long time ago my great master, my best master, he called me Tam.'

'All right, we'll call you Tam too.'

'Poor Tam's a cold,' muttered the boggart, and then: 'What is Humphrey?'

'What? Oh – You mean what does it mean? It – it is the name of a brave man.'

'We thought it suited you,' put in Laura cunningly. 'He used to deal with thieves and bad people too.'

The boggart glowed. He nodded gravely. 'Good. Call me that. The other one is too old, I think. I think maybe worn out.'

'Humphrey, will you tell us about Ally? You know more than anyone.'

He peeped at the children slyly from the corners of his eyes. He began, in his husky voice, to tell his version of the story.

'She is ice and snow. Like a dryad is a tree. She is guarding the treasure. But she has been with a human, she is not only ice. Ice will sit for ever. Ally grows tired, lonely. Her tired and lonely creeps out. It is in the air. No one wants to be near. It is bad for people. Do you understand?'

'A bit.'

'Yes. And my master must help the people. You see, a long long time ago, when there was a town here and everyone was rich, there were three brothers Carey. They were fighting, fighting, who should be the chief of the town. It was the first brother, oldest, who went with the ice lady. She killed every one of the brothers some way or another way. But the younger brothers have family, and when the people find the ice thing stays with them they say it is the fault of this family, though it is not. The town went away, but everybody says the family, that is the Careys, must stay. You must keep her, they say, you and your stupid treasure that nobody can have. Do you see?'

'With difficulty,' said Richard. 'The Careys are descended from one of Prince Karr's brothers, I suppose, one of the two that Ally killed. So it is their responsibility to stop their watchdog from ravaging the countryside.'

'I do not know what about "prince",' said the boggart suspiciously. 'My master is not treasonable. It is a lie. He goes to church – except in the bad weather.'

'All right, all right,' said Richard. 'Whatever he did,

it's been over a long time. We only need to know about Ally.'

'Sssh,' said the boggart, and gave a frightened look at the wall between the houses. 'Listen. My master wanted to cure the land. At last, he conjured her, to speak to her, and to ask: "What will keep you quiet?" She said, "Divide me. Take away my human like me and put it to sleep." So my master did this. He made a poppet, a doll, and it was her asleep. So she can rest.'

He broke off and looked sly again. 'Not *quite* rest,' he whispered. 'Of course. For there is the treasure still. She must know when robbers come.'

'The White Lady!' said Laura. 'Richard, do you remember long ago, Mr Midfirth said the moor was — used to be — haunted?'

'It is her, a little bit. Much better than before. My master put away the words that will make the poppet into A—, her, again. He is the first one to put them away, and so it is very hard. He rested then. He is still resting. Ah, well. Since then, there is only a little trouble, and only when a thief comes. But . . .' He began to shiver again, and huddled against the fire. Richard could hardly make out his words, when he went on to say that the guardian had 'gone wrong'. She had ideas that couldn't be. She would break things. It wouldn't be only thieves. When he first saw her he said, respectfully, most respectfully, 'Good, you have come back', and 'Eat the thieves. I won't stop you', and 'We are the same kind. We stay with our people. We keep our trusts.'

'What did she do? She hit me. Oh poor me and the cold hand.'

'Why, I saw that!' exclaimed Richard.

Laura couldn't understand the mumbling. She had gone back to the window. She was peering between the curtains. Still the snow fell. The road was buried. Nobody could come near Cauld House. Drifted so high, drifted so deep, the snow falls, and falls, and wraps round, and round ... Laura stared into the white dream. 'It is terrible, but it is wonderful,' she thought. 'It will cover the whole world.' Her lips moved: 'Ally ... Ally ... Aster ... Snow ... snow ...'

An ear-piercing shriek startled her awake. Humphrey had jumped up. He was crying:

'Stop it! Stop it! She is reaching you! Close the eyes, close the eyes. They let her in!'

Laura said, 'What was I doing? Why am I by the window?'

They drew the curtains tight again, and sat close together after that, for a while.

'What happens now?' said Richard.

'We wait,' said Humphrey. 'And then they come, and we try to fight. Oh poor me!'

Time passed. At one point the polar bears came snuffling again. The snow had stopped whirling and was falling silently, so they could hear the crunch of footsteps. Somebody rattled at the door and voices muttered. Richard got up and cautiously went to the window, and risked a peep round the curtain. It was a shock to see a round hole rubbed in the snow on the pane: someone had been trying to peer in.

'What are they up to?'

The boggart shook his head. 'It's nothing. They are impatient. *She* is not impatient. *She* does not creep.'

He was keeping Laura amused, at least that was what Richard supposed he was doing. He had made her get out crayons and paper and scissors, and they were both cutting out and colouring flame shapes in red and orange and yellow. Laura was already tacking up the first few, around the door.

'It passes the time,' said Richard dubiously. 'But Humphrey, I'm afraid she won't be fooled.'

'Not now. We fool her later. We need something. When we have it, she will be fooled, maybe, for a little.'

Dr Radleigh was still unconscious. Outside, somewhere behind the clouds of Ally's weather, the sun went down at last, and at once the wind began again. It was the start of the longest night of the year.

About the time that Richard and Laura were putting up their strange decorations, their parents were still trying to get back to Cauld. Dick Pledge had received a confusing message that the children had 'gone back already'. He wasted time waiting at the hotel. By the time he realized something must have happened to Richard and Laura, Ally's storm had descended from the moors and taken over the whole area. It wasn't possible to ride a motor bike through it. He managed to get a lift out to the chemical plant, or at least in the right direction: there was no public transport to Cauld by this time. He managed to reach his wife. They phoned the house on the moor and found that the line was dead. At that point they began to be seriously worried, rather than just bewildered.

They reached Cauld in the dark, just as the snow storm began again. They went to knock up the electrician. No answer. Eventually someone put their head, very cautiously, out of the next house:

'He's not well. He's in bed, poorly. He won't come down.'

'But he was supposed to be at our house.'

The voice said, muffled by the storm, and the shawl

it had wrapped around it: 'Not today.' The door was firmly shut.

In all the village there wasn't a single light, there wasn't a single sign of life behind the doors and curtains. The Pledges' car was not particularly hardy. At the third time of trying to get it on to the snow-buried road to the ridge, it simply died, and would not move. They got out and stared at each other – blank and faceless in the bewildering snow. They saw that there was one light, after all. It was glowing behind the curtains of the stationmaster's office, just across the road at the foot of the hill.

'Ah,' said Mr Midfirth. He was sitting quietly, smoking his pipe in front of a tiny gas fire. He seemed to have been waiting for them.

'Shut the door, Missus. I don't want her in here.'

'Listen,' he said, while they stood dripping and staring at him. 'It's like this. It's a long story. You'd better sit down.'

'Sit down? The children are up at Cauld House in this storm. All we want is to borrow – '

'Ropes and lanterns? You'll never get any vehicle up there now. If you take my advice you'll just wait while it's over. She never harms but the bad 'uns.'

Three figures wrapped in blankets huddled round the paraffin fire.

'When will they come?' murmured Laura.

'Soon enough,' said Humphrey.

He was not talking about rescuers, and nor was she. Richard suddenly said 'I'm cold' and sat up sharply. He had felt a change in the atmosphere. Just then there came a ratatatat on the door. 'Richard?' someone cried. 'Richard?'

'Mum!'

The boggart grabbed Richard's arm and held him down. 'Wait!' he hissed.

Someone began banging on the back door too. They could hear Dad's voice, faintly bellowing through the house: 'Laura! Laura!'

'Wait,' said the boggart. Then a horrible thing happened. Mum's voice began to change. She sounded desperate: 'Let me in! Let me in!' She started to cry. And Dad too, shouting wildly and sobbing. Laura's eyes were very wide. Richard bit on his lower lip. But nobody moved. At last the silence came back.

Down in Cauld, Mr and Mrs Pledge sat and listened to a story.

'Up till forty years ago this place had a right bad name. You may say they were after what didn't belong to them, and it served them right, but it's not nice to have your locality known for mysterious disappearances and people turning up without their wits, or dead of exposure. And the winter weather was dreadful. Well, when the last of the Carey daughters died we took our chance. We got up there before the lawyers. My mum and dad were among the people that decided. We knew there was another branch, but we took the liberty of burning the papers, and then all her stuff went to auction. It's not as if there was money in it, Mr Pledge. We were doing you a favour, really.'

The Pledges were sitting down after all – wondering if the man had gone mad.

'Well, we had peace for a while. Now the trouble's back. Antique shop indeed – up there! We saw through that pair, and we decided to give you a fair deal. Well, I don't know what happened between you and her and them, but it's obvious now, isn't it?'

'We don't understand what you are talking about,' said Mrs Pledge.

'Well, she's taken matters into her own hands. I warned your young Richard that she wanted watching, but you Carey's won't be told.'

Mr and Mrs Pledge understood nothing, except that by now they were very sure that their children were in trouble and in danger.

'Come on, Sally,' said Dick Pledge. 'We'll get *some-one* to help us. And if not, we'll go up ourselves.'

The second attack on Cauld House was more realistic than the first. It began with the distant sound of a car's engine. They heard it struggling and grinding up the snowy road – it was very convincing if you forgot how deep the drifts must be by now. The car drove into the Pledges' garage. Footsteps on the path. Stamping in the porch. Two familiar voices brring and grumbling and exclaiming at the weather. Bang! Bang! 'Open up! Don't keep us hanging about. We're rescuing you!'

Richard got to his feet with a great grin of relief on his face.

'No!' cried the boggart.

'Oh, don't be silly. This time it's real. I can tell.'

'Richard,' said Laura. 'Richard, what about the garage door?'

'It's locked,' said Richard blankly.

'Yes. But they just drove straight in.'

Again they waited, stopping their ears and gritting their teeth, until the lying voices gave up their sobbing and pleading. The silence began again.

It was a long silence. 'Perhaps they have gone for

ever,' thought Richard. He looked over his shoulder. It was very dark now, outside the warm paraffin-smelling circle of light. They had been sitting, dozing and trembling, for hours and hours. 'We're like savages,' he thought. 'Crouched round our miserable dirty little fire. It is pathetic. What can we do against the cold blackness? It is so much greater than we are. It is vast. It is all around us.'

He could not see the familiar furniture – the curtains and the walls and the doors. It was all lost. He shuddered and turned back into the firelight. 'Goodness, it's getting chilly in here,' he said, trying to comfort himself with the sound of his own voice.

'Look at the flame,' said Laura.

It was shrinking and turning pale.

'It is going out,' said Richard flatly. His words sounded like tiny pebbles rattling on a huge sheet of glass. He watched the fading flame, hypnotized. He thought, 'When that goes out, I give up. The cold wins.' He did not care any more. He saw himself leaving the dead fire, standing up, opening the door and making the night outside one with the night inside. Endless snow, endless snow, under an icy moon. It seemed like a good idea. He looked at the two faces with him in the dwindling light. The boggart was like a wasted corpse already. Laura looked haggard and shrivelled, cold and grey. 'The ice has hold of them,' he thought.

Laura was trying hard to do something. She was feeling, like Richard, the cold power, but she was still struggling. She thought that if only she could raise her hand and touch someone, she would be warm again. Richard saw a skinny bluish claw lift itself and reach for him. Laura saw her brother's face twist in disgust – he wasn't Richard any more; he didn't know her. The last light struggled, flickered and died in the fire and lamp. Cold dark closed over their heads. Laura wailed aloud, and at that moment the boggart suddenly came to life and cried:

'Now! Now!' He grabbed hold of both of their hands: 'We have something strong. It is fear. Use it, use it. It is all we have. Make fire!'

'Fire,' thought Richard, so cold he could hardly breathe. 'Flames . . .' He would have jumped into a furnace willingly. He jumped, and Laura must have done the same, in her mind, for he heard her cry out: 'Flames!' Out in the dark room something began to happen. The paper cut-outs were real. They were leaping and crackling: they were glowing red and orange. Fire! Fire! The house is on fire!

'I'm warm!' gasped Laura. 'I really am warm – it's true!'

There was a sound, it was hard to tell where it came from, of retreat. Like a long cold wave dragging back reluctantly from a shingle shore. Something glimmered. All by itself a flame crept back into life in the wick of the paraffin fire. Richard turned up the lamp and stared around at the quiet room. The paper cut-outs dangled foolishly.

'We've won!' cried Laura.

Richard stood up. He crossed the room. This time the boggart did not try to stop him. He kicked aside the little roll of blanket and opened the front door. The night outside was still now. Snow fell like a curtain, but it was silver snow. The moon of the white solstice looked down between the clouds, very bright and hard. With a start, he realized he could see three figures. Only their backs – they were at the end of the path, and walking away. He was suddenly horrified at what he was doing, and flung the door shut on the snowy night. The boggart had come to stand beside him:

'They were on the doorstep! Why didn't they attack me?'

The boggart said, 'She is not impatient. She is playing a game. But it is not playing for us. We have no strength left. We must hide.'

Apparently he wanted them to hide in the cellar, though Richard could not see that it would make any difference. He had the feeling that Ally had finished playing cat and mouse and she would not be so gentle when she next attacked. Moreover, they still could not wake Dr Radleigh.

'We can't leave her.'

'Foolish,' hissed the boggart impatiently. 'She will not let anyone in, will she? You are dangerous to her here.'

'What does he mean?'

'I think we're bound to let Ally in, next time she tries something. Don't you feel it? I'm exhausted. So Dr Radleigh is safer here if we are out of harm's way. We'd better do as he says.'

He made them put on all their outdoor clothes again, because they couldn't take the fire.

'Are we going out?'

'No,' said the boggart. 'We are going *in*.'

When they got to the cellar he began to pass his hands over a part of the wall, while the children stood on the steps with the lamp.

Laura stared. 'It's my door,' she said.

'Yes. Secret door. Only for the Careys. Quick, quick. It is my master's door.'

He hurried them through it and down a flight of stone steps that wound away, deep underground. They came out in a round little room that had once been panelled in wood. There was a high press with enormous books mouldering in it. Everything was crumbling and rotten. But in front of the tall cupboard was a desk, and at the desk somebody was sitting, with head buried in arms.

'Oh,' said Richard and Laura.

Humphrey smiled: 'Ah, my Master.' He went over and gently smoothed the tumbled black curls. The man had fallen asleep, worn out by his long work. He had fallen asleep a very long time ago, and no one had ever disturbed him. The brow that Humphrey stroked was pale as ivory. Mr Carey's eyes were very deep and dark.

Richard took the lamp and help it up. He wondered if Dr Radleigh had known about this secret place. She had 'sealed' the cellar, but she hadn't suggested they hide in it. Why not?

There were some papers on the desk. Richard peered at them. He read:

'My imp, my bold Tamburlaine, the great warrior, is such a timid soul I fear me he'll be but little use. But my sister has the paper, and will pass on the secret . . .'

'Hey, Laura, it's his diary. Come and look.'

But Laura was still standing by the stairs. Her head was turned, as if she was listening to something.

Richard read a few more words of the diary. Then his eye was caught by something darker than a shadow, half hidden by a rotting curtain in the curve of the wall.

He held up the lamp again. It was another door. He heard Dr Radleigh saying: 'The way to the treasure is through the house.' Suddenly he knew why she had not brought them down here: 'We are the danger!'

He turned round. The chamber was empty but for Humphrey, sitting at the bottom of the steps, looking guilty.

'Laura! Humphrey, where has she gone?'

'She went for candles,' said the boggart. 'The lamp will not last long.'

'What? And you let her go!'

Without waiting for an answer, he crossed the room. But the boggart would not let him pass:

'No! No! They've got her. You can't help her. You stay with me. You're the Carey one. You keep us safe.'

But Laura was just as much a Carey as Richard. There was already candlelight coming down the stairs, and footsteps. Laura was first, looking bewildered and frightened. After her came Tom and Edith – and Ally.

11   *The Promise*

It was a barrow, that had been built underground. The second stair, from Mr Carey's study, came in at one end. Down the length of the chamber you could see that there had once been a long shape built out of stone – a narrow shape with a high curve jutting at either end. A stone ship. It was half buried in a roof fall of rubble and crumbling old earth. The lamp and candles caught glimmers of a vast cavern outside. Somewhere out there must be the river, locked in ice, cracking out of its course and giving the world above its first faint taste of Ally's power. Tom had tied the children and the boggart to the stone prow of the ship.

'No wonder that house is draughty,' whispered Richard, 'with this great hole underneath it.'

He could faintly see the side of Laura's face, trying to smile. He was relieved that she had come out of that horrible daze at least. None of the three of them had resisted at all, in the end. The boggart was just hopeless as soon as he looked at Ally; Laura was out of it; and Richard was cursing himself, realizing that Ally had meant all along that her cat and mouse game would force them to hide, *further in*. Dr Radleigh had known. It wasn't Laura's fault. It was inevitable from the beginning. So Edith grabbed a child in each hand; the boggart got a *look* from Ally, and simply crawled, and down they all came to the secret centre of the house, the end and the beginning of the story. Tom was last, struggling with two huge suitcases down the narrow winding stair.

The treasure was just lying in a heap on the floor, as if someone had abandoned it in flight. It was all gold. Far-travelling mercenary warriors had brought back flasks and cups and jewellery, inlaid with enamel and gems, from Mickelgarth – Byzantium. There was red gold from raids on the Welsh and Irish coasts, twisted into heavy torques and bracelets. There were richly decorated hilts of weapons that had lost their iron blades. The beauty of this trove was that it was a sea robbers' hoard to start with. They would be able to sell it piecemeal, and no one would ever guess it came from one great find. Tom and Edith counted over the goods with their eyes, but they didn't touch anything. They did not dare – not yet.

There was a shadow over the gold. It was the shadow of a woman. It seemed to be made of blue glass; it had sharp edges but no depth. It lay on the treasure, its arms spread. One of its shadow hands was curled over a thick necklace, like the thing the lord mayor wears. It was the only thing in the pile that was not gold; it was only silver. But once it had been worth all the rest.

Richard thought of a little nation of retired pirates, trying to be farmers. The 'king' of a few square miles didn't wear a crown, that was just romancing. But it was not just romancing that the spirits of the great icy north were somehow still near these exiles, even on Cauld Moor – the shadow on the gold. He said softly to Laura, or to himself, 'She's been here all along. Wherever else, always here as well. All these years.'

Laura did not answer. She was listening to Tom and Edith.

They were discussing what to do about the old lady they had found lying upstairs. They couldn't understand how she had got away from the car crash. Tom wasn't sure. Maybe there'd been no crash. But Edith was quite certain.

'She was injured, but she somehow managed . . . ' They were going to carry her out and leave her by the road in the snow, near her own car if that looked reasonable. 'Someone'll find her. Bound to,' said Tom. It was already decided that the children and the boggart were to be left as they were.

'They can shout for help, can't they? Anyway, they'll have those ropes undone soon enough when we've gone. I didn't make much of a job of it.'

'No need to worry then,' said Edith.

They could shout, but who could possibly hear? And Richard and Laura already knew about Tom's knots. They were hard and tight. Twisting and straining only made them worse. It was horrible, standing in the cold gloom, and listening to this slippery dialogue. Behind the Shores, a tall pale figure stood against one of the broken walls. Her head was bowed, as if she was overcome by the memories of this place. But Richard had the impression she was smiling, as the Shores whispered. He was far more afraid of *her* than the other two.

'Laura,' he said. 'I want to apologize. It's all my fault. You're right, I just don't want things to happen, so I look the other way. I knew all along there was something *very* wrong about Ally. I knew the first day we came here. We're in this mess probably strictly because I didn't want to look a fool.'

'That's all right,' said Laura. 'No one would have believed you. *I* know.'

But now there was a new development. The Shores had remembered that the mysterious door up above was a Carey secret. Perhaps they needed a hostage, to pass through it again. 'Be a nuisance,' said Tom. They decided to try first if something belonging to a Carey would do the trick. Edith was already taking things out of her handbag, and laying them out, ready to start the ceremonies she thought would set Ally's shadow free, to join Ally. Tom rummaged in his pockets and brought out a pair of nail scissors.

'Hair?'

'That sort of thing.'

Tom advanced on the children, the little scissors perched on his finger and thumb.

'Fight?' hissed Laura.

'May as well give them as much trouble as we can,' muttered Richard.

They began to yell and struggle: 'Go away! Go away! Leave us alone!' To their surprise the boggart, who had been just snivelling helplessly, suddenly started bouncing against the cords and yelling too. He squealed: 'Master, master! Oh! Come quickly!'

Tom had been merely grinning at the children's row, but at this he stopped. He had seen the boggart's 'Master' on the way down. Supposing that Mr Carey up there, all made of ivory as he was, had really come to life? The boggart stopped squealing. So did the children. For now the sounds Humphrey had heard were closer and clearer. There was someone coming down the stairs. Everyone, including Edith, turned and stared.

The limping, uncertain footsteps came down and down. Tom, looking distinctly worried, moved so that the children were between him and the door. But it was not the ghost, or the walking bones of the dead magician. Out into the chamber stepped a slight, stooping, elderly lady. She did not have her glasses. She was carrying her shoes in one hand, and a handful of crumpled paper in the other. She looked battered, unimpressive, and rather confused.

Tom said, 'I knew we shouldn't have just left her there.'

Edith said, 'Deal with it', and went on with her preparations. But Tom didn't move. There was something rather ominous about that old lady. She was still just standing at the foot of the stairs, but her eyes were on Edith, and at a second glance, she didn't look confused at all.

'Edith Shore. Are you trying to raise up that shadow?'

Edith turned round. Her mouth dropped open.

'Don't you realize the folly of it? You may get ahead of the storm tonight, you two, but what about tomorrow? The blizzard we have seen is just the faintest reflection of what Ally will do when she is whole. Don't you remember? "The bones of the earth will crack and break." Ice will tear up the land. There'll be a hundred, a thousand blizzards. We may never see spring again. What use will gold be, in a world like that?'

The children held their breath. It seemed impossible that Edith would go on with her plan. But the Shores were not impressed. Something like a wink passed between them. They were not quite stupid enough to want Ally loose, at any price. Dr Radleigh saw them smirk at each other. She said: 'Oh, I see. You mean to lift the shadow and immediately conjure Ally back into her doll shape, shade and all. You never meant to keep your promise!'

'Hey!' said Tom, alarmed. 'Keep your voice down.'

'Don't worry.' Dr Radleigh looked over their heads at the creature like a tall fair woman, standing in the shadows, waiting. 'I am giving nothing away. She knows. Edith Shore, you know very well that your "magic" is petty and ineffective at its best. Think about what has happened since you began this. The height of your achievement was to give a child a head cold, and a bad dream or two. *How could you* be in control of a creature like Alvilda? She has been laughing at you all along. You didn't bring her here. She brought you. There is no need for your "ceremonies", Edith. The shadow will leap from the gold the moment a thief touches the treasure. That is the arrangement. *That* is why Ally needs you to set her free.'

For a moment it seemed as though Edith understood. But there was no saving the Shores from their greed. Both together, it dawned on them that Dr Radleigh had said they only had to touch the gold. Tom lunged. Edith grabbed. There was a cool laugh from somewhere.

But in the same moment Dr Radleigh, who had tried her best to persuade by reason, spoke again. This time she spoke in Latin (Richard thought). Whatever it was, the two thieves immediately crumpled up and fell to the ground. Dr Radleigh swiftly snatched up the knife from Edith's properties, came to the children and began cutting cords in a great hurry.

'Are they dead?'

'Asleep.'

'What happens now?'

'I don't know. The thieves are very near the gold, and the moon is still high. I am afraid we may have lost — unless we can talk Alvilda into laying down her freedom willingly.'

The children, released, stumbled and rubbed at sore wrists and numb ankles. The boggart, on his hands and knees, began to sneak off to the stairs. But he stopped and began to wail. It was too late to run away.

Something was happening to the shadow. It was moving. Its faceless head seemed to be raised, as if it could smell the thieves. And its arms and legs were stretching over the rock and through the air, like the arms and legs of a shadow that dangles from your heels at the end of a summer's day. It was reaching towards Alvilda. Dr Radleigh said:

'You will have freedom. But nothing else.'

The ice spirit watched her shadow growing towards her. She answered: 'Ice and snow will not spoil the world for me. And if I kill everything I touch I will be no lonelier than I have been for a thousand years. Must I sit forgotten in this stone box for ever? I cannot die. Nothing will ever change. I *will* be free.'

Dr Radleigh said, 'It is not true that nothing will ever change. But even a single night seems endless if one cannot sleep. I can take away the weary watching. I can make you sleep, and not wake until the morning when time ends.'

The shadow hands stretched out. Alvilda did not move away from them. But she was hesitating. Richard could see that she was wavering.

'I have been put to sleep before. I had bad dreams.'

Of course. That was what Mr Carey, the one who sat upstairs, had done. He'd deceived her. He did not want to give up his watchdog entirely. Richard was so caught up in the drama he forgot about all the danger, even the danger to himself.

He jumped forward and cried, 'But it isn't the same. We don't care about the gold. This time it is real. We won't disturb you – ever.'

At once, he wished he had not spoken. For the creature turned and *looked* at him. Her eyes on his face seemed to parch the skin and shrivel the flesh against

153

the bone. His face felt scoured and stripped, the way the world outside would be, when Ally was in power. She was so cold, she burned. She said: '*Why should I believe you?*'

Standing in her breath was like standing in a bath of ice. Richard, shuddering and wincing, pushed his hands into his pockets while he mouthed for words that wouldn't come. His fingers closed on something in the right-hand pocket.

'Because, because . . .' he gasped, helplessly. He heard Dr Radleigh take a deep breath, heard her whisper: '*Yes*, Richard. Remember who you stand for here. She would listen to *him*, surely.'

Someone had given him something on the moor. He took the thing out, and looked at it. He had been wearing this anorak out on the moor, in the snow. On his palm lay a crooked root of heather, and wound around it was a twist of bog-cotton, like a lock of pale hair. It was a sign, but he didn't understand it. He looked at the little token. The ice mist of Alvilda's breath was making his head spin. He was holding the little thing out to her. He wondered why. He heard his own voice saying, 'Because you promised.'

Then there was confusion. He thought he saw Dr Radleigh, hustling Laura and the boggart to the stairs. There was a voice, reading aloud more of the story of Prince Karr. The candles turned upside down. The blue shadow danced on a golden ceiling. Someone took the token out of his hand . . .

Could that have been Ally? 'Well, it was all very mixed up,' thought Richard. He sat up and swung his legs over the side of the bed. Was it a dream? He shook his head. It was crowded with strange fragments — the senior mistress from school doing magic, a pile of gold. 'And Laura was in it, and we were stranded, and oh yes, the boggart.' He looked out of the window. It was a fair morning, and tomorrow was the last day of term. The moor was bare and brown – no hope of a white Christmas.

'I'm late,' he thought. And there he was brought up with a jolt. He could not remember yesterday at all. He knew what he ought to remember – carols at the cathedral, and the Rutland hotel. But his head was still buzzing with that powerful dream.

'But what am I doing back here?'

Maybe the whole hotel business was a dream as well. He put on his dressing-gown, noting absently that his room seemed unusually warm for a change. He thought a wash might sort him out. But on the way to the bathroom he met Laura, standing at the door of her room.

'My window's broken,' she said.

They stared at each other, in each of their faces a strange question. Then, from downstairs, there came a burst of laughter. Visitors? At this time in the morning? They rushed down to the kitchen, and there was Dr Radleigh, sitting with Mum and Dad, eating breakfast.

'Hallo,' said Dad. 'Fine pair of stranded arctic explorers you are. You slept all through our superb rescue! We had such a time getting up here last night. It was incredible. Nobody would help us. You should have heard Mum – making speeches about you poor lambs, stranded up here. Then finally we all set off in the middle of a blizzard, on foot, in the middle of the night . . .'

'Feeling most intrepid . . .'

'And the joke was, by the time we got to the top of

the ridge *not* only was the storm over, and the night as quiet as a Sunday school picnic, but the blessed snow started melting!'

'Worse. *Not* only were you asleep in bed, but you'd never been alone at all!'

'We didn't even have any mince pies to give them. We were so embarrassed.'

The joke and the excitement of the blizzard story covered many things. Richard found himself being told it was very wrong of him to get Dr Radleigh to drive him and Laura back here: 'You couldn't help the blizzard, but whatever you'd forgotten it was hardly so very important. Look at all the trouble you've caused Dr Radleigh.'

Dr Radleigh said she didn't mind. 'A little liveliness is good for a quiet old lady,' she explained, straight-faced.

Laura choked on her tea. 'Mum!' she said, to cover her confusion, 'have you put out Humphrey's milk yet? Can I do it? Can he have some toast?'

'*Toast?*'

Richard went to the front door with Dr Radleigh. The moorland air was cool and mild. They were looking for the breakdown van, coming from Sope to deal with Dr Radleigh's poor car.

'It is all *gone*,' said Richard.

'Of course,' she said. 'February is the time for snow in England. Not December.'

Number Three seemed to be deserted. Richard said, 'Are they gone too?'

'They drove away,' said Dr Radleigh. 'They won't come back.'

'And Ally? And the treasure? And . . .'

But Dr Radleigh was shaking her head. 'No, Richard,'

she said, 'No wondering. No discussions. We made a promise, don't you remember?'

'What?'

'To leave someone in peace.'

The breakdown truck arrived, and Dr Radleigh drove away with the man from the garage. Richard was left alone on the doorstep, gazing out at the calm and secret moors. After a minute or two, somebody in the house called 'Richard' and he went inside, and shut the door.

THE BEWITCHING OF ALISON ALLBRIGHT
Alan Davidson

Alison has always sought refuge in day-dreams: of a lovely home, of being an exciting person, of doing all that the others at school do – and more. Dreams ... until Mrs Considine appears, spinning her amazing web of fantasy, creating another life for Alison out of those dreams. There is no magic in the bewitching of Alison Allbright, only the hypnotically dazzling lure of that other life. Until it's clear enough to see clearly.

STAN
Ann Pilling

Stan couldn't have been more unlucky in running away from his London foster home, for he gets unwittingly caught up in the activities of vicious criminals and is pursued by one of them who will stop at nothing to get what he wants. But throughout his terrifying journey to Warrington and Liverpool and across the Irish Sea, Stan never loses hope of the determination to find his brother and the home he dreams of.

DREAM HOUSE
Jan Mark

For Hannah, West Stenning Manor is a place of day-dreams, but for Dina its attraction lies in the celebrities who tutor the courses there. But when a well-known actor arrives, hotly pursued by his attention-seeking daughter, Julia, Dina begins to realize that famous people are no better than ordinary ones. A warm and tremendously funny story by the author of *Thunder and Lightnings*.

BOSS OF THE POOL
Robin Klein

The last thing Shelley wanted was to have to spend her evenings at the hostel where her mother worked, when all her friends were going away for the summer holidays. Then to her horror, mentally handicapped Ben attaches himself to her and although he's terrified of the pool he comes to watch her swimming. Despite herself, Shelley begins to help him overcome his fear.

ROB'S PLACE
John Rowe Townsend

Rob thinks he'll never be happy again. Everyone is deserting him: first his dad, then his best friend, now even his mum hasn't time for him with a new husband and baby. Finding everyday life more and more difficult to cope with, he discovers Paradise – a fantastic place which is all his own and where he is master. But can he manage to control his fantasy or will his Paradise become a nightmare?

THE WELL
Gene Kemp

Living in a Midlands village in the years before the Second World War with her parents, her much-loved brother Tom, and three grown-up sisters, Annie (alias Gene Kemp) finds life full of surprises and fears, disappointment and delights.